Lock Down Publications and Ca$h Presents

I0666776

The Lane 3

Written By
KEN-KEN SPENCE

First Edition 2025

Printed in the United States of America

This is a work of fiction. Names, characters, places, and incidents either
are products of the author's imagination or are used fictitiously. Any
similarity to actual events or locales or persons, living or dead, is
entirely coincidental.

Lock Down Publications
P.O. Box 944
Stockbridge, GA 30281
www.lockdownpublications.com

Like our page on Facebook: Lock Down Publications
www.facebook.com/lockdownpublications.ldp

Stay Connected with Us!

Text **LOCKDOWN** to 22828 to stay up-to-date with new
releases, sneak peaks, contests and more…

Like our page on Facebook:
Lock Down Publications

Join Lock Down Publications/The New Era Reading Group

Visit our website:
www.lockdownpublications.com

Follow us on Instagram:
Lock Down Publications

Email Us: We want to hear from you!

Dedication

Like always to Lil Chris and B-Dub. Two of the realest nigga's that ever walked the streets of Dallas. Rest in peace. Also to the Creator for blessing me with this opportunity.

Long Live The Mandingo's

To The Readers

What's up, y'all? First and foremost, I want y'all to know that this was the hardest book I ever wrote. I had to overcome many obstacles to finish this book. I want to apologize to Cash and the whole LDP family and thank y'all for having patience with me. I got burned out on Omar/Short Dogg. He done sold all the dope he could sell and fucked all the ho's he could fuck, so what's next? I really had to get creative and try to come up with some material that y'all would enjoy. I hope I did that. But, I'm in prison and I'm trying to get a lot of anger and shit outta my system. I'm trying to get a lot of anger and shit outta my system. I'm not ashamed to admit I'm not all the way there yet. So, I broke my hand punching a nigga in his shit, and as soon as my hand healed enough to where I could get back to writing, I had to punch another nigga in his shit and rebroke my hand again.

Don't judge me, I'm trying, (LOL). Anyway, I gotta tell y'all a little about myself and give y'all some working information as to my experiences. I'm serving life for murder and I'm not happy all the time. Sometimes I get depressed and it's hard for me to write without what I'm feeling coming out in these pages. I've been through hell and back. They said I wouldn't see 18. But, the devil a lie. Guess what? Ken Ken done wrote three books and I'm just getting started. Book 4 is coming real soon and it's going to be a little different. But, this book is from my heart and this one is for my Mama. I had to write something that she could read.

5

I autographed Book 1 and 2 and sent them to her, and she read book 1. I was so ashamed. It's too much fucking and killing in those books.

Man, my Mama can't read no shit like that. She's a Christian woman trying to live her life for God. So, book four is her. I'mma keep it gangsta, but I had to switch it up a little. When I'm writing these books, I feel everything I put my characters through. I almost killed Shalika in book 3, but I couldn't do it. I had fell in love with her and got depressed thinking about killing her. So, I hope y'all enjoy this book. I read some of the comments on Amazon from the people who have read book 1 and 2, and thank you for the positive reviews. I hope I can continue to write stuff that y'all like. Don't be scared to write me and tell me how you feel. Visit my Facebook page, Ken Ken Spence, and leave a comment. Thank y'all for rocking with me and know that I'm grateful and appreciative that I can continue to entertain y'all with these hood tales that y'all spend your hard-earned money to buy. Thank y'all.

Ken Ken

Chapter 1

Omar sat on the dock of the yacht in some red Polo shorts, soaking up the sun rays. He thought about all that had happened in the last month. Ole man Santos had finally made contact with him while he was out at a steakhouse with his family and security detail, including Pecas and Chief.

They were all sitting at the table when the waiter came over and told Omar that a Mr. Santos was in the back and requesting his presence.

"You might as well get it over with," Pecas said.

"Might as well. Come on, let's go see what he wants. Em, you come with us." He looked over at J-Low and K-Rock and said, "Don't let shit happen to my family."

"Understood," K-Rock said.

They stood up, and the waiter said, "I think he wanted to talk to Mr. Wilson alone."

"We go wherever he goes," Chief said. "Let's go."

They went to a back room where the ole man was sitting at a table alone. Three bodyguards were strategically sitting around the room.

"Hey, Omar, it's finally nice to meet you," Mr. Santos said, smiling and sticking his hand out. Omar shook his hand.

After they sat down, Omar asked, "What did you need to see me about?"

"Well, first, I wanted to commend you on the wonderful job you did for my old friend, Enrique. I was wondering if you would like to continue the arrangement you had with him at a cheaper price?"

"I don't want to waste your time, but I'm retired and happy to stay that way. I'm enjoying this time with my family. So the answer to your question is no. There's a lot of money I need, and I got out with my freedom and no Feds sniffing around asking questions. I'm not willing to test my luck again, so I'm going to turn down your offer."

"I think you are making a mistake. But I will respect your decision for now. Contact me if you change your mind."

"Will do." Omar got up and left the room with his crew right behind him.

Now, as he sat soaking up the sunshine, he couldn't help but wonder how long it would be before the old man came at him on some aggressive shit.

Rudy warned him before he left the country to be careful and not relax. Chief and Pecas wanted to start shit off and not just sit back like some ducks. But Omar was reluctant to start a war with the Santos clan when war hadn't been declared by either side.

He knew you couldn't make money while at war. They still had a warehouse full of work to get off of. Guns, gunshots, and dead bodies brought heat, and he had run his empire without the laws in his business so far. He wasn't on the Feds' radar, and he wanted to keep it that way.

Zell came out on the deck and sat in his lap. "What are you thinking about?"

"I forgot when I saw you in that bathing suit." She was wearing a white two-piece that showed her heart-shaped butt. She'd gotten a suntan that had turned her body golden brown and matched the blonde highlights in her hair.

They shared a long kiss. "Thank you, baby. You make me feel pretty and beautiful."

They kissed again. Omar slid his hand under the bottom of her swimsuit and caressed her clit while pinching her nipple through her top. She moaned in pleasure.

"Let's go inside," she whispered.

They went inside to the master suite and made love for an hour in the middle of the Atlantic Ocean. It was the first time they had been able to spend any meaningful time alone in a long time.

They went back on the deck after showering together and sat down, enjoying the sun. Sando, the waiter, came and asked if they wanted something to drink.

"Bring us a bottle of wine," Zell told him.

"Coming right up."

Omar had almost dozed off when he heard the familiar sound of a bullet striking flesh. He opened his eyes and saw Zell covered in blood and Sando half-laying on top of her, with half of his head missing. He grabbed Zell and carried her inside, the whole time looking around at the other ships in the area, trying to see where the shots came from.

"Nooooooooooo!" he screamed, holding Zell in his arms. Pecas and Chief came running.

"What happened?" Chief asked.

"Somebody fired some shots from one of those boats," he said, pointing. They both pulled out handguns and ran out on the deck to look.

When he looked back down at Zell, she was staring at him. "Oh shit, you're alive." He grabbed her and hugged her. "You were shot, baby. Are you in pain?"

"No, I feel fine. My head hurts a little."

He ran and got a wet towel and started wiping the blood off her. He checked her whole body but couldn't find any bullet holes. She had a small knot on her forehead, but that was it.

"Damn, I thought you were shot. I saw all that blood on you, and I thought . . ." He couldn't even finish the sentence.

"The last thing I remember is Sando falling on me, and we bumped heads."

"I'm glad you're all right," he said, hugging and kissing her. "Tell them to take us back to the house," he told Pecas.

9

He pulled out his phone and called Em and told her what happened and to get everyone inside and away from the windows.

"They tried to hit my wife," he said, seeing the picture clearly. "Sando must have leaned over to set the wine bucket down just as they fired the shot and took the bullet that was aimed at Zell."

"I was thinking the same thing. I just didn't want to say it," Pecas said.

"They fucked up. I was trying to be a businessman, but they won't let me. Now I'm 'bout to murk everything they love."

Chapter 2

The doctor was leaving from checking on Zell as Omar was finishing up his last phone call. He'd called the whole crew down to Florida—Big, Dre, George Jay, Dell, Glenn, Dub, D-Money, Bobi, Slime, Robert, Smurf, Yakki, and Junior. Pops and Faye were coming also.

He walked out with the doctor.

"She'll be alright in a couple of days. She has a mild concussion. Give her a couple of days of rest, and she'll be back to normal."

"Alright, Doc. Thank you for coming," Omar said as he slipped a wad of bills in his hand.

"Anytime. Call me if anything happens."

"Okay, Doc."

Omar went in to check on Zell. Shalika and Yolonda were sitting on the side of the bed talking to her.

"How are you feeling?" Omar asked.

"I feel fine."

"The doctor said you need rest. I'm going to go check on the kids. I'll be back later."

"Okay."

He went down the hall and found Danielle entertaining Shayla, Lil Omar, Omari, and Omahji. They were watching *Shazam*—even the babies seemed to be enjoying the movie.

"Hey," they answered.

"Is Mom alright?" Danielle asked.

"Yeah, she's good. Just resting. Y'all alright?"

"We're good, just watching a movie."

11

"Well, I won't bother y'all. Enjoy the movie," he said, hugging each one of them and kissing the babies.

He left the room and went to the back dock where Em was standing with a pair of binoculars, watching every ship she could see. She had an AR-15 laying beside her.

"Where is everybody?" he asked.

"J-Low and K-Rock went to meet one of her old CIA buddies to pick up some equipment."

"To check the house for bugs. Listening devices? So you think they might be listening to us?"

"I wouldn't put it past them."

"Everybody is on their way down here—the whole crew. We finna crank this shit back up and murda the game. Them muthafuckas tried to touch my wife. That was the wrong thing for them to do. That white woman is off limits. They fucked up," he said, walking off with his head down.

Em's panties got wet. She loved that gangsta shit, and she had already witnessed Omar's gangsta. The last time he got mad, he chopped a nigga's head off and took it to the nigga's best friend's son. Shit was about to get ugly, and that's exactly what she and her girls had been trained for—the ugly shit.

Let's get it, she thought, caressing her AR while staring out at the water.

Omar went to his office and sat down behind the desk, thinking. Something wasn't adding up. He wanted to be sure he was doing the right thing going at Santos. The man hadn't made any threats or demands—he had simply asked Omar to get back in the game and work for him. He never made any threats or appeared to be angry when Omar told him no.

Omar pulled out his phone and dialed the number that old man Santos had given him.

"Hey, my friend," the old man answered.

"Somebody took a shot at my wife and killed one of the workers. Everyone pointing the finger at you," Omar said— not one to be beating around the bush.

"Son, I can assure you that it was not me or any of my people. I want you to work for me. I don't want to harm you or any of your family. Don't listen to the rumors that are being spread."

"I was told that you had Enrique killed."

"I had nothing to do with Enrique's death. We were business partners at one time for many years. We had a difference of opinion on how to move forward, and we agreed to split. We were still cordial, and we split on good terms."

"I heard a recording of my housekeeper telling you where Enrique would be spending the weekend. I hear her voice—and I know that voice. The same voice told someone that I would be coming to Florida."

"I'm sorry to inform you that you have fallen for the oldest trick in the book—and it's easy to do when you are dealing with people you think you can trust. But, Son, you never heard my voice on the recording. I never talked to Marie about Enrique's whereabouts because I knew where he would be. I was already at the villa waiting on him to arrive. We were talking about getting back together. How do you think I know so much about you? Enrique told me—and he wanted me to meet you. His own people killed him. I never wanted him dead—we were childhood friends. Maybe they killed him because they didn't want us to join forces again. Or maybe someone wanted to be the man. I don't know, but I can promise you that I had nothing to do with any of it."

"So who do you think might have orchestrated it?" Omar asked.

"Several people could have done it. Freddy is a stand-up guy—I wouldn't suspect him. Pecas is a leader, but he's not ambitious enough to want to run the whole show. Chief is not a leader—he's just a hothead. If I had to take a guess, I would say Rudy. His father is Mexican cartel, and they resented Colombiana coming in. But they needed our product, so they needed us. But that's who I would suspect. Watch closely—a snake always shows his fangs."

After they hung up, Omar sat back thinking about all that the old man told him. He called Em and told her to come to his office.

A few minutes later, she was there.

"What's up? Are you alright?"

"Yeah, I'm good. I think something strange is going on. I just got off the phone with Old Man Santos, and he told me that he didn't send anyone at us—and he had nothing to do with Enrique's death."

"We heard the recording."

"We heard Marie. We never heard who she was talking to. Think about this shit for a minute—Santos has never sent anyone to follow us. Pecas and Chief came from Rudy's people."

As she sat, contemplating all that he had told her, K-Rock walked in with a black box in her hand with a long antenna on it.

"What's that?" Omar asked.

"This is a listening device detector. If a bug—that's what we call listening devices—was in here, the needle on this screen would move," she said, waving the box around the room. "We good. I've checked the whole house."

"One of my friends that I was in the Agency with works down here. They got all kinds of shit."

"Hey, you think she can listen to somebody's phone calls?" Omar asked.

"Yeah, that's easy. Who you trying to listen to?"

"Chief and Pecas."

"What's going on? I thought they were on our side."

"We did too, but some new developments have come up," Em said.

Em went on and explained to her what was going on, and when she was done, Omar said,"We just want to make sure ain't no snake shit going down. You know I hate snakes."

"Me too," K-Rock said.

"Me three," Em said.

"Let me call her and see if we can get this done." She left the room, pulling out her phone.

"I feel some fuck shit in the making," Omar said.

"You might be right, but the question is why they tryin' this on us now?"

"Old man Santos says it's behind money. I was their biggest distributor, and they can't stand missing that money we were bringing in. If they killed Enrique, then it's somebody not satisfied with their position. They wanna be the man."

"Who you think it can be?"

"Rudy."

K-Rock came back in and said, "She's going to come over tomorrow and set the recorder up. She said we have to have a safe place where she can set the recorder up. It will record, and we can go back at a later date and listen. You don't have to be sitting there listening like in the movies."

"We can use one of those rooms in the attic. Nobody goes up there," Omar said.

"Well, she'll be here tomorrow."

Chapter 3

Faye, Pops, the boys, Connie and her husband Smurf, and Trina, Robert, Lisa, Dub, D-Money, Bobi, Slime, and Yakki all decided to drive because Faye was taking King and Queen with them. They were six cars deep.

They drove for two days, taking stops to let the dogs use the bathroom and drink water. They spent the night at a pet-friendly motel and the next day drove the rest of the way.

When Faye finally saw the house, she said, "This damn house is big as a shopping mall."

"And it sits right on the ocean. Omar is stacking some major bread," Pops said.

"Yeah, he is doing that. But he better sit his ass down before them alphabet boys be at his ass. I plan on talking to all they asses about that while we are here too," Faye added.

"I hope they listen. We all know this shit don't last forever," Pops said, pulling up to the front of the house.

"They gon' listen, 'cause they know I'm not driving up and down no highway to no prison visiting room."

Everybody was outside waiting when they got out of the car. King and Queen jumped out as soon as Faye opened the car door and ran and tackled Shayla and Lil Omar. They tried tackling Danielle, but she was too smart and big for them.

"Hey, Granny Faye," Shayla and Lil Omar said, giving her a hug.

"Hey, how my babies doing?" she asked, giving them a hug.

"We alright," they both answered.

"I know Mama Faye ain't the only one out here y'all see," Jay said, getting out of the truck.

"Naw, that's all they see," Glenn said. "So I can put my presents up."

"No, no! Give me my present, Uncle Glenn!" Shayla said, jumping on his back.

Lil Omar joined in, and before long Glenn had both of them in the air.

Shayla was having so much fun she hadn't even noticed Smurf get out of the truck he was in. When Glenn put her down, Smurf snuck up behind her and grabbed her in a bear hug, kissing her cheeks.

"Smurf!" she screamed when she saw who it was.

"Hey, baby girl."

"I missed you. Can you stay with us for a while?" she asked him, hugging him.

"I'm going to stay with you for a while. That's why I'm here."

After everybody said their hellos and they started to go inside, Faye asked, "Danielle, where is your mama and daddy?"

"I think they upstairs taking a nap."

"I bet they is," Faye said.

***

While everyone was downstairs having a reunion, Omar was upstairs laying long dick to Shalika, Zell, and Yolonda.

He had come upstairs from his morning workout to find the three of them having an all-out fuck fest. Shalika was eating out Zell, Zell was eating out Yolonda, and Yolonda was eating out Shalika.

"Come on over here, baby," Zell told him when he walked in the room.

"Let me take a quick shower," Omar had said, running to the bathroom.

THE LANE 3 | KEN-KEN SPENCE

He came out the shower and went back in the bedroom still dripping water and buried his dick in Yolonda's pussy.

It had been years since he'd had some of her hot pussy and he couldn't wait. He banged her back out until Shalika pushed her off the dick and jumped on it. He fucked her to several orgasms and finally got to Zell.

He put her legs on his shoulders and slow-fucked the shit outta her while Shalika and Yolonda watched and cheered them on.

"Oh shit, I'm finna cum," Zell moaned.

"Me too."

"Cum all over that dick," Shalika said, sticking a finger in Zell's ass while Yolonda sucked on her breast.

"Oh shit, I'm cumming," Zell said as her pussy started squirting.

As soon as Omar started nutting, Faye started beating on the bedroom door.

"Y'all bring y'all nasty asses outta there right now! You got company downstairs and we ain't gon' be sitting down here while y'all up here fucking!"

"Mama, we was sleep," Omar said through the door.

"Boy, stop lying! I been standing here listening to y'all's nasty asses. Knock that shit off and get downstairs!"

"Yes, ma'am," all four of them answered.

They all jumped in the shower together and took a quick shower. As Omar was drying off, he saw two pregnancy sticks wrapped in a red bow. He picked them up and saw they were both positive.

He smiled and asked Zell, "Whose are these?"

"One is mine and one is Shalika's."

He grabbed Zell and Shalika, and they all started hugging and kissing.

"I love y'all so much," he told them.

"We love you too," they both said.

"Ooh, look at that dick — it's hard again," Shalika said, reaching out and stroking it."Yolonda, come suck his dick and make it quick before Mama Faye come back up here."

***

Twenty minutes later, they all came downstairs. Omar greeted everyone, including King and Queen, who almost knocked him to the floor. He saw Faye glaring at him from her seat. He walked over, gave her a hug, and kissed her on the cheek.

Then he handed her the two positive pregnancy tests. She was so happy she was about to have two more grandkids, she forgot she was mad at him.

He took them out on the yacht and let them see the ocean. They left the women on deck, and the men went inside to talk about getting back in the game.

Chief and Pecas were on deck watching every ship that came close through binoculars, with high-powered rifles nearby.

They didn't know they were being watched. Omar and K-Rock had hired a whole new crew for the ship and new staff for the house as well.

As soon as they got ready to start the meeting, Faye walked in and said, "Excuse me, I need to talk to my boys for a minute."

All five of them looked at each other, then got up and followed Faye outta the room. Pops already knew what was coming, so he stayed seated and let Faye handle her business.

"Look, y'all need to make this your last run. I'm not going to spend the rest of my life visiting one of y'all in a prison visiting room. Y'all have been lucky so far."

As she was talking, in walked Shalika and Zell.

"Y'all are the mothers of Omar's children," Faye said, addressing Zell and Shalika. "Stop being passive and express to him how y'all feel. Because if something happens to him, then y'all gon' be raising kids without their father."

"And Omar, you are the head of the operation — so when you say it's over, it's over. Stop letting your brothers and friends make you feel guilty about their financial situation. Every one of them should have enough money saved up to be comfortable for the rest of their lives. It's not your fault they messed their money off at the strip club, buying expensive cars, or whatever they did. You did your part — you gave them the opportunity. They don't have families. You have the most to lose. Your wives and kids depend on you and need you. So think about that. I'm done. Y'all can go on back to your meeting."

***

After the women left, they sat there for a minute. Omar was thinking about what Faye said. He couldn't stand the idea of being locked away in a cell away from his kids and the two women in his life.

He made up his mind right then — he was through.

If the rest of the crew wanted to keep going, he would plug them in with Old Man Santos and see if he would do business with them. But as for him, he wasn't touching another drop.

Glenn finally broke the silence.

"Bro, Mama right. You got too much to lose. Whatever you decide, I'm rocking with you on it."

"Yeah, real talk," Jay and Dell agreed.

"What about you, Junior?" Omar asked his baby brother.

"Man, I manage clubs and shit like that. Y'all niggas is the gangstas."

They all burst out laughing.

"Come on, let's go back in here," Omar said.

Chapter 4

Tyrone 'Brazy T' Jackson walked out of the Dallas County Jail three months after he had been bench-warranted back for a new trial. He had gotten his murder case overturned on appeal, and the prosecutors had decided not to retry him.

A lot of the witnesses from the first trial had been reluctant to come back to court and testify again. So, they had no choice but to let him go.

He stood in front of Lew Sterrett County Jail, sucking up free air. Period. He had to immediately check in with his boy, Short Dogg. He had come through for him. He got him an attorney to work on his appeal, sent him money to his prison account, and checked on his kids and his no-good-ass baby mama to see why she hadn't been staying in touch. Period. He also made sure his kids were straight on school clothes and the things they needed every year he'd been out.

Tawanna, his baby mama, had already moved another nigga into the house that he had paid for. He wanted to ask Short Dogg to run the nigga off, but he knew he couldn't act like no lame-ass nigga in front of the big homie or make a bitch keep it real with the nigga that was locked in a cell hundreds of miles away. So long as the nigga wasn't abusing his kids, he was straight.

He took a taxi to North Park Mall so he could buy an outfit and get out of the outdated prison clothes they gave him. He had a little over five stacks that were on his prison account, so he was straight for a minute on cash.

He went in the mall and bought underwear, T-shirts, socks, four outfits, a few pairs of shorts, and two pairs of J's. His last stop was the Metro PCS store, where he got a cell phone. He went outside and got another taxi to the house he'd bought for him, his kids, and Tawanna.

They pulled up in the hood, and he had the taxi driver park a couple houses down. A group of little boys were playing football in the street. He immediately saw his son but didn't spot his daughter.

He paid the taxi driver, grabbed his bags, and got out. Trey, his son, saw him as soon as the taxi pulled off.

"Oh shit, that's my daddy," he said before running and jumping into Brazy's arms. "You home, man, I missed you."

"I missed you too, lil nigga. Where your sister at?"

"She in the house on the computer, where she always at."

They were twins and had just turned eleven. "Come on, let's go see her." They took off walking to the house.

"Trey, come on, nigga, we beating these niggas' asses," one of the boys said.

"I gotta go, nigga. I'll be back later."

Brazy walked in the house and went to the room where his daughter was on her tablet. He snuck up behind her and put her in a bear hug.

"Trey, get yo' ass off of me before I kick your ass," she said until she saw Trey walk in front of her.

Brazy finally let her go, and when she saw who it was that had her in a bear hug, she said, "Oh shit!" Then she realized she had cursed in front of her daddy and covered her mouth.

"Don't just sit there, give yo' daddy a hug," Brazy said.

She jumped into his arms with tears in her eyes. "I missed you so much, daddy."

"I missed you too, baby girl. But I'm back now, and I'm not gon' ever leave y'all again. Where yo' mama at?"

"She in her room sleep. She work at night."

"Let me go holla at her. I'll be back in a minute."

He went down the hallway and quietly opened the door. He went in the room. Tawanna was lying on the bed, butt-ass naked, half-covered by a sheet, asleep.

He thought to himself, even if she was a sorry bitch, she was a fine-ass sorry bitch. She was light-skinned with hazel eyes, 38DD breasts, and 46-inch hips. The bitch was fine; he couldn't deny that. And even after having two kids, she didn't have one stretch mark or baby fat left on her body. He felt himself getting hard.

He went over and locked the bedroom door, stripped down to his birthday suit, and eased into the bed behind her. He wrapped his arms around her. She scooted back up against him. He started to gently massage her clit. She let out a soft moan but continued to lightly snore.

After a minute or two, he eased his fingers inside of her and felt her wetness. He removed his fingers and placed his dick at her opening, easily sliding inside her warm wetness. After all the years of being locked up and deprived of sex, it took everything in his power not to nut.

He lay there for a minute, buried inside her, and got himself under control. Finally, he started slow stroking in and out of her. She arched her back, giving him more access to get deeper inside of her. Now he was fucking her long and hard while still massaging her clit.

"Ooooo, shit, that dick feel so good," she moaned.

"Who pussy this is?" he asked, pounding her back out.

"It's yours, Tyrone. It's all yours. It's been yours since the day you popped my cherry. Oh, shit, I know this dick anywhere, even in my sleep I know this dick. Fuck this pussy!"

"This dick good to you?"

"Oh yes, I missed this dick so bad."

"Why you give my pussy away then if you missed this dick so much?" he asked, getting mad at the pussy and trying to kill her. He was fucking her so hard.

"I just needed to cum! This yo' pussy, baby, and you know it. Oooo shit, I'm finna nut. Fuck me harder!"

"Cum on this dick. Let that shit out," he told her, still pounding her back out.

"I'm cumming! I'm cumming!" she screamed, throwing it back at him.

***

In the other bedroom, Trey and Kay heard the moans of their mother and father's lovemaking.

"You hear that? Daddy in there fucking the shit outta mama."

"Boy, you nasty. They gon' be doing that every night like they used to."

"She ain't never made no noise like that with that nigga Ricky."

"I wonder where Ricky gon' stay now that daddy home?"

"Daddy probably kick that nigga ass, then put him out."

"I hope they don't get in no fight. Ricky cool. I like him, but he ain't Daddy," Kay said, laughing.

Back in the other bedroom, Brazy was still fucking the shit out of Tawanna. All of the years of built-up anger were gone as soon as he put his dick inside her. He'd told himself for years that he would never fuck with her again. But all that changed when he saw her fat ass and titties in live and living color.

"Oh shit, I'm 'bout to nut in this pussy," Brazy said, pumping in and out of her.

"Oooo yeah, cum in this pussy, fill this pussy up with that hot-ass nut!" Tawanna urged him on, throwing it back at him.

He finally busted inside her with an orgasm that started at his toes and went all the way up his body to the top of his head. It felt like he shot twenty pounds of cum in her pussy. He collapsed on her back, out of breath and barely able to move.

"Damn, baby, that was good," Tawanna said, turning over and guiding his head to her breasts. He remembered that she always used to like for him to suck her breasts after they had sex.

He started sucking her breasts for a minute before he snatched away and got up, looking around for his clothes, mad at himself for fucking her.

"What's wrong?" she asked, seeing his mood change.

"I told myself I wasn't gonna fuck with you no more after the way you treated me while I was locked up."

"Boy, you tripping. So you telling me that you wouldn't have fucked no other bitch if I had went to prison?"

"I ain't said shit about you fucking no other nigga. We got two kids together, and we been together since junior high school. You could have at least wrote a nigga and brought my kids to see me."

"I could have did a whole lot of shit different, and you could have too. But all the shit is over. You at home now. Let's not dwell on the past, let's work on our future."

"That's over with. I will always love you 'cause you the mother of my children, but you not the type of bitch I need in my life. You ain't that ride-or-die type of bitch. You the kind that's only gonna be there when shit going good. But when shit get ugly, it's on to the next one with you," he said, putting on his shoes and leaving the room. He went down the hall to Kay's room, where he left his bags with newly purchased clothes. "Let me use your bathroom to shower, baby girl," he told Kay.

Tawanna lay in the bed with her pussy still throbbing, knowing that what Tyrone told her was true. She had trust issues with men. She'd watched her mom and dad cheat on each other every chance they got. Just like her mom, she was a sneaky, conniving bitch when it came to men.

She smiled, knowing how easy it was for her to run game on Brazy and play him outta some dick. A few moments ago, she was standing at the window, looking out when she saw the taxi pull up and saw him get out. She'd hurriedly got undressed and got in bed, playing sleep. She positioned herself so that when he walked in the bedroom, he would see her fat ass and the big, juicy lips of her pussy.

One thing she knew for sure, being a woman had taught her: *a hard dick had very little conscience, if any at all.*

Chapter 5

"I'm not going to get back in the game. I called y'all down here 'cause I was finna get us a drop and lock the city down again. But, my plans have changed in the last few minutes. Both of my wives are pregnant, and my kids need their father, so I'm not ready to take any more penitentiary chances. Now, I know some of y'all ain't as well off as some of us, and we a crew, so I can't shine and not let my people shine too. So this is what I'm gonna do. I'ma get the plug to fuck with me, and I'ma let D-Money and Bobi run the business if they want to." He looked over at them.

"Hell yeah, we down with that," D-Money said, and Bobi echoed.

"I know my brothers are out the game too. Dub, you out too, so don't even think about it. Dre, what you gon' do?"

"If you out, I'm out."

"So, Smurf, Robert, and Lisa, Slime, and Yakki, all y'all niggas gonna be took care of. Bobi, you and D-Money gotta stay on these niggas' ass. Violence don't do nothing but bring the police around and get niggas locked up. So, men, we need you niggas to keep that in mind."

"Bro, let me get the girls?" Bobi asked.

"Who you talking about?"

"K-Rock, J-Low, and Em."

"That ain't gonna happen. Next question." They all busted out laughing.

While they were talking, Omar's phone started ringing. He looked at the screen and saw it was a Dallas area code and answered.

"What's up?"

"What's poppin', blood?"

"Who is this?"

"This Brazy T, nigga!"

"Where you at, nigga?"

"I'm out. They let me out a few hours ago. I'm at my baby mama's house."

"Nigga, come to Florida. I got the whole clique down here with me. George, Big Dre, D-Money, Bobi, and Dub."

"I'm with my kids. Tawanna gon' let them come stay with me."

"Nigga, bring them too. Look, I'm finna get my peeps to get you three plane tickets. I'll call you back with all the info in a few minutes. This yo' number?"

"Yeah."

"Alright, I'ma call you back when I get the info," he said, ending the call.

Omar went out the room and called Zell and Shalika. He told Pops and his mom,

"I just got off the phone with Brazy T. He out and on his way down here."

"You talking about Tyrone, little badass, Sharon's oldest boy?"

"Yeah, baby, call and get three reservations on the next plane for him and his kids," he told Shalika.

"Queen, call the bank and get them to give him a bank card with a hundred stacks on it. His name is Tyrone Jackson; he'll be by to pick it up before they close," he told Zell.

"Is this the guy we got the lawyer for?" Zell asked.

"Yeah, that's him."

"That's good, they were able to get him out," she said, pulling out her phone and calling the bank.

He went back in the room and told Bobi and D-Money, "Y'all hold a spot for this nigga Brazy. You already know that nigga gonna be trying to get at that bread. I might put that nigga on some more shit since he bringing his kids with him. We'll see once the nigga get here and we get him settled in. I'm trying to be back in Dallas within the next thirty days. I have fell in love with the ocean, but I miss the city. Ain't nothing like Dallas. Back to what we were talking about, I'm only going to do this for a year so y'all can get your bread stacked up. So, if in a year you don't have your bank right, that's on you. All that extravagant spending and shit ain't what's up. Save your money and invest your shit in some legal shit. That's what I'm looking to do, find some more businesses to get involved in."

"Short Dogg," Lisa said, "You ever thought about a record label? You already know Robert done had hits before, and you might not know this, but Lil Smurf go hard on the mic too. Him, Robert, and my two kinfolk you met at the spot in the south got a group they started, and they been making some hot-ass songs."

"Them niggas don't go hard like that," Dub said, messing with Rob, really trying to get him to spit something.

"I got a CD of one of the hottest songs they made a couple of weeks ago. Let me go get it." Lisa stepped out and came back a few minutes later with the CD.

Short Dogg got up and went to the system and put the disc in. The beat started off with the sound of a freight train in the background, then the bass dropped with a sick-ass beat. Then Lil Smurf came with his verse.

"Freight train comin' / Big shoes on / Running through this bitch, nigga stomping / Nigga stacking money to the ceiling / I ain't really got no feelings / I don't like niggas or bitches / I don't really like nothin' livin' / Wrist on froze / Chain got the whole room cold / Lil' bitch seen all that ice / Thought she was in the North Pole"

Short Dogg sat back listening to the song and thought to himself, them niggas had some skills. He already knew Robert was nice on the mic. He made up his mind right then to hurry up and get them niggas outta the trap and in the studio.

"What y'all want the name of the label to be?" Short Dogg asked.

"MOB Records. What else?" Lisa answered.

He was thinking that he might have just stumbled on a gold mine with the music. But he was almost sure that Lisa was going to be just as valuable to his team with her hustling skills. He sat back and watched how she promoted their music and knew he had to hurry up and get her a position somewhere on his staff.

Chapter 6

Later that night, after they'd ate dinner and were sitting around having drinks and passing blunts, Glenn asked the question that had been on everyone's mind.

"Lil' Bro, we've talked about how we're going to proceed on the business side of things. But the real question is, what we gonna do about these fools takin' shots at my sister-in-law? I ain't gonna just let that kind of shit go, and I hope you ain't."

"That's the craziest shit I ever heard come out your mouth, my nigga. You know damn well I ain't finna let shit go when niggas done shot at somethin' that belong to me, and that white woman belong to me from the bottom of her feet to the top of her head. Whenever I get some solid info on who responsible, I'ma make him feel me. My team workin' on that as we sit here enjoyin' this evening."

"You don't have any idea who it could've been?" Jay asked.

"Yeah, I do. But we don't want to make any premature moves and hit the wrong people. Trust me, we on top of it, and in a few days we should know what's goin' on and who's responsible. Now, with that bein' said, let's talk about somethin' else," Short Dogg said, turnin' to Shalika and askin' her if she got the plane tickets.

"Yeah, I already called him and gave him the info. They leave from Lovefield Airport at 11:20 tomorrow morning."

"He already got the card too, from the bank," Zell added. "While you were still meetin' with your brothers, I got his number from your phone and called him with all the info."

"Okay, thank y'all. This is what I wanna do. I'm tryin' to buy about a hundred cheap houses and fix 'em up and resell 'em or rent 'em out. I wanna buy some apartment complexes and do the same thing. Em, would y'all be interested in bein' over that?" He asked, lookin' over at Em, J-Low, and K-Rock.

"Yeah, we can do that."

"Okay, y'all come up with a name for our company and call the info to Shalika so she can do the paperwork and go to the banks with it."

"Lisa, I want you to do the same thing with the record label. Find a building, get the equipment you need, and get back with me ASAP. I want you to run this shit if that's cool with your hubby," Short Dogg said playfully, lookin' at Robert.

"That's cool with me as long as she at home by bedtime," Robert said, and they all laughed.

"Junior, find us some more buildings so we can open some more clubs, sports bars, or whatever."

"Bro, I got an idea that I been thinkin' about for a minute," Junior said.

"Run it down to me and see if it's a good one or not."

"Look, I was thinkin', Glenn got the Red Door in the South. He been had his spot for years, and that bitch be packed. Glenn just finished that culinary arts school, and you know him and Jay think they some chefs. Let's find a building downtown and open the Red Door #2, three floors: a bar on the first floor, a private club on the second floor, and a restaurant on the third floor with Glenn and Jay as the chefs."

"Junior, that's the dumbest shit I ever heard," Short Dogg said, lookin' at Junior like he was crazy. "You know not one of them niggas can cook," he said, bustin' out laughin'.

"Fuck you, lil' nigga." Glenn said, laughin'.

"I second that fuck you," Jay said.

"Naw, naw, I'm just bullshittin'," he said in between laughs. "I think that's a good idea. What you think about that, Glenn?"

"That's a good idea. That'll give me and Jay somethin' to do now that we retired from our other business," Glenn answered.

"Yeah, but we gon' all put in on the cost to get everything set up and rollin'," Jay added.

"That's cool with me," Omar said.

"I'm puttin' my half in too. Plus, I'ma be the manager," Junior said.

"I'm good with all that as long as the place make some money," Omar said.

"I'm good with it too," Jay added.

"Me too," Glenn finally said.

"Okay, now that that's settled. What kind of plans you got, Dell?" Short Dogg asked.

"I was gonna see if Lisa needed some help with the record label."

"I don't have a problem with that," Lisa said.

"Okay, well y'all handle that shit," Omar said, turnin' to Zell and Shalika. "Did y'all find us another house? I wanna be back in Dallas by next month."

"We found a nice place right outside of Dallas off Cedar Creek Lake."

"Did you buy it?" he asked.

"Not yet. I wanted to look at it online and tell me what you think," Zell told him.

"I trust you. Do you and Shalika like it?"

"Yeah, we both think it's nice. It has a huge main house and six guest houses. The whole property can sleep forty people. It has a private boat dock and over 500 feet of open lakefront."

"Buy it so we can get back to the city," Omar said.

33

"Okay, but it's ten acres. Can we defend that much property?"

"Call a security firm and get them out there to put up cameras, electric gates, and motion sensors. Did you get the check from the insurance people for the house?"

"Okay, okay, I'll buy it. It's already furnished too," Zell said over her shoulder, leavin' the room.

That don't make no difference, he thought. *Y'all still gon' buy a bunch of shit we don't need.*

Chapter 7

Pecas answered his phone without looking at the screen to see who was calling.

"Yeah."

"I need you and Chief to go over to the house and take over things," Rudy said.

"This Rudy?"

"Yeah."

"Man, where you been?"

"I had to make a few runs. But look, I need you and Chief to get over there and take over things down there."

"Freddy got that under control."

"Freddy is no longer with us. Everybody that was there is gone. That's your operation, I need you to get over there and set up. Get your own people in there."

"What's goin' on? Where's Freddy?"

"I'm taking over. Freddy has been removed."

"What you mean removed?"

"He's dead, 'P'. My grandfather started this family, it was meant for me to be in control of it. I need you and Chief to handle things for me down there. I trust you guys and know that things will be ran correctly. Once I get everything in order, I'm going after the Colombians."

Pecas sat back, listening to Rudy, shaking his head. "Rudy, you are crazy. Power is ruining what we had. We had a nice operation, and you are destroying it on a power struggle. We were marijuana guys before the Colombians. We became billion-dollar cartels because of the Colombians.

Now you wanna start a war with them? I can't be a part of that. I don't trust you anymore, Rudy. I would be looking over my shoulder every day, wondering when I would be next. I just put it all together—you killed Enrique, you took a shot at Omar's wife, and if it wasn't for Sando, she'd be dead—"

"That was an accident," Rudy interrupted.

"You don't make accidents shooting at people's family. Now you have killed Freddy. How many more, Rudy?"

"I was just trying to get Omar back in the game on our side. We need that production. That bullet wasn't planned to hit anyone. Sando got in the way."

"Sando was doing his job, Rudy. That bullet was never supposed to be fired. Now you have lost Omar. He's back in the game, with Old Man Santos. I can't help you now, Rudy, you have lost it," Pecas said before hanging up the call.

He was still sitting there in a daze an hour later when Chief walked in the room.

"What's up, 'P'?"

"Rudy called."

"What did he want?"

Pecas explained everything to Chief that Rudy told him. "I'm not getting involved in the bullshit Rudy is doing. How long will it be before he has someone shoot us in the back?"

"Yeah, I feel you on that. Rudy's gone mad. So what we gonna do?" Chief asked.

"We are gonna stay right where we at and get this money with Omar and his family."

"Man, you might not have noticed, but the nigga been acting real strange since the shooting with his wife—like we had something to do with the shit," Chief said.

"Nah, I noticed it too. But, I'd be the same way if someone had taken a shot at my wife. Nigga don't know who to trust," Pecas admitted.

"So how we gonna work with or for a nigga that don't trust us?"

"I'm just gonna go to him and let him know everything that Rudy is up to and see how the shit play out. If he don't want us on the team, then shit, we both got enough money saved up to where we can open a business or something."

"Whatever you decide, I'm with it."

Pecas got up and left the room to go have a talk with Omar.

After his talk with Pecas, Omar and K-Rock listened to the recording of the conversation. They saw that Pecas was on the up and up.

"I'm going over to that house where they at and see if Rudy is there. If he's not there, then his people gonna feel me the same way one of my people felt him," Omar said.

"You know I'm with whatever you decide. We gonna take the whole crew, or is it just me and you?"

"Let me holla at 'P' and see what the setup is at the spot— how many people there and all that. I might take him with us and let him put in some work to see if he really down with us or if he faking."

"I'm ready whenever you are," K-Rock said, getting up to leave. "Hey, you think we can listen to that nigga Rudy's calls?"

"Yeah, I'll get the number and start monitoring his calls."

"Alright. Hey," he said, stopping her before she could leave the room, "you wanna go with me to pick up my nigga from the airport? We can leave a little early and make a few stops."

She smiled a little because she knew he had already read her mind. "Yeah, that's cool."

"Alright, we on."

She walked out the room with a little more bounce in her step.

Omar called a meeting with his brothers and laced them up on what he had found out. "So basically, the nigga was just trying to get me back in the game. He wanted me to think that Old Man Santos was the one doing the shit. That way, he could kill two birds with one stone. Get me back in the car with him and get me to take out Santos at the same time."

"That nigga Rudy think he slick, huh?" Jay said.

"Yeah, but he gotta come better than that to get me. The whole time, I've had Pecas and Chief's calls being monitored. Every time they got a call, we listen to every fucking word. So, you niggas give me some credit and know that I'm on top of my shit."

"Lil' Bro, it ain't like we questioning you or your moves. But, nigga, you are our little brother, and mistakes cost niggas their lives in this game. So, iron sharpens iron. We in this shit together—you hurt, we hurt; you eat, we eat. So don't ever think we against you. We just crossing all the T's and dotting all the I's, ya dig?" Glenn told him.

"Nuff said right there," Dell added.

"I'm finna go to the airport and get Brazy. Y'all niggas take care of the house while I'm gone. I don't think we got shit to worry about, but don't get caught slippin'. I'm finna send Em and P over there to the spot where Freddy was at to see if they can spot Rudy."

"We got this shit. Go on and handle your business," Jay assured Omar.

Omar told J-Low and Em what they had found out and told Em to take P with her and go do some surveillance on the house where they met Freddy. He told J-Low to stay and watch the house. Him and K-Rock took a Suburban and left to go to the airport to pick up Brazy.

As soon as they were on the highway, Omar reached over and started rubbing K-Rock's pussy through her shorts.

"Ummm," she whispered seductively, gripping the steering wheel harder.

"You plan on stopping somewhere so I can handle this?" he asked, continuing to massage her clit through the material of her shorts.

"Yeah," she answered.

"You better hurry up, 'cause I can't wait," he told her, unbuttoning her shorts and sticking his hand inside her panties to rub her clit.

"It's . . . a . . . motel . . . right . . . up . . . there . . ."

She hurried to the exit and drove into the parking lot of the motel. She grabbed her purse and jumped out the truck to go get the room. A few minutes later, she came back with a key card.

"Let's go, we are in room 10, right there." She pointed.

As soon as they got in the room and closed the door, Omar pushed her down on the bed and took her shorts and panties off and started eating her pussy.

"Omar . . . I . . . need . . . dick," she moaned.

"Let me taste this pussy first. You taste like pineapples," he told her in between licks on her clit.

After a few minutes, he finally undressed and pushed inside her.

"Ummm," she moaned. "Beat it up, baby, don't play with it."

He pulled her to the edge of the bed and pushed her legs up against her chest and pounded her back out.

"Oh shit, just like that. Just like that!"

He put her on her knees and hit her from the back. They fucked like animals for an hour before they finally got in the shower, where Omar hit her from the back one more time with warm water running over them.

Finally satisfied, they showered and left the room to go to the airport.

Chapter 8

Brazy stepped through the tunnel with his twins right behind him. He saw Omar smile and head his way.

"What up, big homie?" he said, grabbing him in a bear hug.

"Ain't shit, glad to see you free, my nigga," Omar told him.

"Hey, Uncle Omar," Kay said.

"What's up, Kay? You alright?"

"Yeah, I'm good."

"Uncle Omar, can we go to the beach?" Trey asked.

"Damn, lil' nigga, you ain't gonna speak first?" Omar asked, playfully throwing a jab at him that Trey easily weaved.

"Oh yeah, what up, unk?" he said, giving Omar a hug.

"This your wife?" Brazy asked, looking at K-Rock.

"Naw, this my bodyguard Kelly. But we call her K-Rock."

"Your bodyguard?" Brazy asked skeptically, looking at K-Rock again.

"Yeah, nigga, my bodyguard. And she got two sisters that work with her. They family and stone-cold killers."

"Naw, for real, fam, stop playin'," he said, looking at Omar. He saw the expression on Omar's face and added, "You dead-ass serious, ain't you?"

"Dead-ass and they deadly."

He turned to K-Rock and said, "How are you doin'? I'm Brazy T, but everybody calls me Brazy."

"I know who you are. Omar talks about you so much, I feel like I already know you," she said, shaking his hand.

"Man, let's get this luggage and get the hell outta here. Where Big Dre and George at?"

"They at the house. I had a few runs to make before I came, so I left before they got up."

They got the luggage and headed out to the truck, driving back to the house. When they pulled up to the gate of the house, Brazy said, "You stay in this big-ass house?"

"I told you, my nigga, we gettin' some real money now. Ain't no more of that nickel-and-dime shit."

They parked and went inside. Big Dre and George were waiting on them. As big as Brazy was—and Brazy was about six-foot-two and over two hundred and fifty pounds—Big Dre grabbed him in a bear hug and lifted him off his feet.

"You free, my nigga," Dre said.

"I'ma be dead if you don't stop squeezin' the air outta me, fat-ass nigga," Brazy said, laughing.

"Glad you free, my nigga," George told him after Dre put him down.

Dub came over and hugged his childhood friend. "Damn, nigga, you got big as fuck."

"Yeah, this all muscle too," Brazy said.

"Fat-ass nigga, you ain't worked out a day you was locked up," Omar said.

"Sho didn't," Big Dre said.

"Y'all niggas hatin' 'cause I'm ripped up," Brazy joked.

They all burst out laughing.

"Tyron," Faye said, walking into the room. "Lookin' like yo' ugly-ass daddy."

"Hey, Mama Faye," Brazy said, giving her a hug. "You know I look good," he added, laughing.

"I'm glad you are free. I hope you can stop shootin' people so you can stay out."

"Uh, yes, ma'am. I hope so too. Where Bobi and D-Money at?" Brazy asked.

"They had to go back to the city. They'll be back in a few weeks," Omar told him.

"I already got you a condo you can have. It's already paid for," Big Dre told Brazy.

Zell, Shalika, and Yolonda walked in the room as they were talking. "These are my wives, Zell and Shalika, and our friend Yolonda. Y'all, this is my friend Brazy," Omar said, introducing him.

"Hey, Brazy, glad that you're home," Zell said, giving him a brotherly hug.

"Thank y'all so much for your help. Omar told me all that y'all did. You found the lawyer, Zell and Shalika. You took my kids shopping every time they needed something. Thank y'all."

"It was our pleasure," Shalika said.

"Come on, let me show y'all your rooms so you can put your stuff up, and then we can go chill and talk," Omar said.

"Just like the penitentiary—come on back to the dayroom. You got all night to unpack," George said, and they all burst out laughing.

Chapter 9

Back in Dallas, Bobi was getting everything high together before the drop arrived. He knew he had to do it because D-Money was lazy and weak behind hoodrat bitches. He kept some kind of drama going with one of his hoodrats. D-Money was his best friend, but Bobi knew his faults and weaknesses. This was their time to shine, so Bobi knew he had to put together a solid crew to pick up the slack for his homies when they started slipping.

The first thing he did was call a meeting with all the young niggas that they fucked with on the Lane. It was already understood that their area of operation would be on Forest Lane.

They were in a one-bedroom apartment in the Palms. All the lil' niggas from the hood were there: Slime, Lil Mob, Lil Bro, Plex, Corey, Kool, Marcus, Zay, Ray, CJ, Blu Jay, Keion, Bobi, and D-Money. Bobi was lacing them up on how they were going to operate.

"We finna take the lane back over. But this time, we gonna do this shit without all the shooting and killing. Whatever an outside nigga try to come on our block and sell, we just gonna make our shit bigger and cheaper until we starve the nigga out and he gotta move if he wanna eat. We ain't gotta be killing niggas when we got all the dope. All that stuntin' and shit, buying expensive cars, drawing heat, and making it hot? You gonna get kicked off the team. We tryin' to stack this paper for as long as we can, get rich, and get out the game. Ain't nobody trying to end up in the Feds.

Lil' Mob, Lil' Bro, and Zay, y'all a team. Plex, Ray, and Keion, y'all a team. Marcus, Kool, and CJ, y'all a team. Slime, you take Corey and Blu Jay."

Bobi spent the next few days getting apartments in several different locations around the area. They still had the spot in the back of the Palms; that was gonna be the headquarters. Slime was gonna be who they went through. Bobi had already decided that he was through with the hood.

He was the head of the operation, and there was no need for him to still be hanging around in the hood. He had workers now, so he could focus his attention on expanding the brand legally. He knew the shit wasn't gonna last forever.

While Bobi was in Dallas making plans, Omar was in Florida about to get some payback. Omar, K-Rock, and Chief got in the Suburban and met P and Em at the house they were watching.

"What's up?" he asked after P and Em got in the truck with them.

"Same thing. It's two or three people in there that we have seen."

"P, call the house and get us in," Omar told him.

P picked up his phone, dialed the house, and spoke to someone for a few minutes. When he ended the call, he told Omar, "Let's go." When they pulled up to the house, the gates were opening.

K-Rock drove up to the house and parked right outside the front door. They all got out, and the front door opened, where a short, stocky Mexican that Omar had met last time he was here was waiting on them.

They shook hands and followed him into the house to a room where two other Mexicans were playing a game of pool.

"Where's Freddy?" Omar asked.

"Freddy is no longer here. I am in charge now," the tallest one said, sitting behind a table.

"What about Rudy?"

"He's outta the country right now. But maybe I can help you. Is there something you need?"

"Yeah, maybe you can," Short Dogg said, pulling out his gun and shooting the Mexican that met them at the door in the face. Then he turned and shot the other Mexican that was standing up in the face also.

Everybody in the room was shocked except P. Pecas pulled out his gun and shot the two Mexicans that Omar had just shot in the head.

"What's your name?" Omar asked the last one.

"Hector," he answered in a shaky voice. "Is all this necessary?"

"Call Rudy," Omar ordered.

"I don't have a direct line to him. I just page him and he calls back."

"Well, page him 911."

Hector did as he was ordered, and a few minutes later his cell phone rang.

"Answer it and put him on speakerphone," Omar told him.

"What's up, Hector?" Rudy asked after he answered.

"Rudy, this is Omar, bro. You fucked up when you took a shot at my family. You should've respected my decision. Now you got a whole lotta me to worry about. You know me, and you know how I get down."

"That was a mistake, Omar. Freddy acted without talking to me. That's why he got what he got. But to make it up to you for the inconvenience, Hector has something for you. Hector, give Omar the bag I left for him. I hope this shows how sorry I am, and I hope we can move on from this without any drama. I sincerely apologize."

"Yeah, we'll see," Omar said, ending the call.

Hector got up and opened a floor safe, then gave Omar a bag with five million dollars in it.

"That's five million dollars," Hector told him.

THE LANE 3 | KEN-KEN SPENCE

"Yeah, I'll take this into consideration," Omar said, catching Em's eye and nodding.

Em immediately pulled out her gun and shot Hector in the head three times. He crumpled to the floor, where Chief and Pecas hit him with three more shots each.

"Let's get the fuck outta here," Omar said, tossing the bag to K-Rock.

Chapter 10

Slime was at the corner store on Forest Lane and Audelia. He was sitting behind tint in his brand-new Range Rover, checking out the activities on the Lane.

Bobi and D-Money had slowly turned over the operation on the Lane to him and moved on to focusing on expanding the empire. He made a few changes to how things were run, and one of the things he liked to do was just sit and watch the block. You could always tell who was who and what was what by laying in the cut and watching who was hanging out with who and who was coming and going. So, that's what he did—sit back behind tint and watch.

It was the summer, and niggas and bitches were everywhere in all kinds of little skimpy attire, hangin' out. Slime was a baller, so he knew all he had to do was step out of his truck, and he would have his pick of any of the bitches hanging out.

But, he had been around Short Dogg too long and knew not to trick his dick off on any hood rat bitch that didn't have anything going for herself. He stayed ducked off in his ride, just checking out the action.

He saw a pink Benz pull up and knew immediately that it was the new chick on the block that everyone had been talking about. He watched as she got out of the car and went into the store. He was too far away to tell what she actually looked like, so he got out and walked to the store.

Slime knew he was a fly nigga and he was on paper. He practically ran the dope game on the Lane, but he wanted something other than the hood bitches and sack chasers.

He walked into the store and saw her standing at the DVD stand, checking out what they had to offer. He was shocked at how pretty she was.

She was tall for a woman, standing about 5'8" or 5'9". She had Asian blood in her, her eyes were slanted, her hair long, black, and silky. Her skin was the color of honey. She was wearing a sundress, so he couldn't tell what her body was like, but her breasts were not too big and not too small. She was wearing sandals, her toes were freshly pedicured, and her fingernails were freshly manicured.

He looked over her shoulder and saw that she was reading the cover of a movie called *Triple D.*

"That's a good movie," he said, walking up on the side of her and looking at some of the DVDs.

"Is it really good? Some of these movies, the covers look good, but then the movies don't be good," she said.

"Yeah, I know, right. I got played by the cover so many times and the movie be straight trash. But that movie right there is really good."

"How many times did you watch it?" she asked, looking up at him.

"Two or three times. I can't remember, but why you ask that?"

"'Cause if you only watched it once, it wasn't good," she said, smiling.

"I watched it a couple times. By the way, my name is Shawn, but everybody calls me Slime," he said, sticking out his hand.

"I'm Im Yo Chick," she said, shaking his hand.

"You wanna be my girl already?"

"Naw, boy," she said playfully, punching him in the chest. "That's my name. My first name is Im, my middle name is Yo, and my last name is Chick."

"Oh, Im Yo Chick, that shit sexy as hell. What are you mixed with?" he asked, staring at her.

"My mom is Chinese and my dad is black, straight off the Lane."

"So, you from around this way?"

"Not really. We lived over this way when I was young, but we moved away. I just recently moved back to the area. I'm in college at SMU."

"Oh yeah? What you studying?"

"I'ma be a lawyer."

"That's real," he said as they headed to the cash register with the movies they chose.

"I hope these movies good," she said.

"Come on, I'ma show you that you gonna like them," he said, pulling her to the register and paying for the movies.

They went outside, and he pulled her toward his truck. "My car is over here," she said, pointing toward her car.

"I know, but I wanna show you something," he said, hitting the key fob to unlock his doors.

"This your truck?"

"Yeah, get in the back."

When they got in, he tore the plastic wrapping off one of the DVDs, put it in the CD player, and pushed a button on the console. A huge screen dropped from the ceiling of the truck, and the movie started playing.

"You think you a player like that, huh?" she asked, teasing him.

"Naw, I just wanted to watch the movie with you, but I thought it was too soon to invite you over to my place or ask to come over to yours. So, this was the only other option."

Thirty minutes into the movie, they had both dozed off.

Chapter 11

"Man, these muthafuckin' detectives keep calling my phone, talking about they want me to come in and talk to them," Big Dre was telling Omar as they sat in the den of Omar's new house on Cedar Creek Lake.

"What they wanna holla at you for?"

"Some kind of way, they got my license plate number off some cameras in the area where that undercover pig was working. They sayin' it's just routine, and they investigating everybody that was in the area the few weeks before the fool came up missing. But, like I told the detective, I don't know shit and haven't seen shit, so I don't wanna talk about nothin' that ain't got shit to do with me."

"Get you a lawyer and go see what they talkin' about. They can't tie you into nothin' that went down, so just to get them ho's off your back, go see what they talkin' about," Omar told him.

"Man, fuck them pigs. I ain't finna talk about nothin' I don't know nothin' about. If a nigga sit down and talk to the law, then he the law. 'Cause nine times outta ten, he gonna say some shit he shouldn't have said, and if they catch you in one lie, then that's when they got a nigga."

"I feel you," Omar said, not trying to keep going back and forth with Dre on the subject. He knew from prison how stubborn Dre was, and if he had already made up his mind, couldn't nobody change it.

"I took all the money I had to the spot and gave it to Glenn. I'ma chill for a little while until this shit blows over."

"Yeah, that's wise."

"If anything happen, he got the money to get me a lawyer."

"If anything like that go down, you already know I'ma get you a lawyer," Omar assured him.

"Yeah, but I still don't want them takin' my shit if they search my place."

"Alright. I wasn't thinkin' about that."

Two weeks later, Dre, Rob, Chief, and Pecas were on their way to check out some property when Dre looked in the rearview mirror and saw that they were being followed by an unmarked police car.

"Hey, the laws are behind us in that white Caprice," Dre said.

"I see them ho's," Rob said, sitting in the front passenger seat while looking out the side mirror.

"I ain't goin' to jail," Dre said.

"Fuck that, I'm ridin' out with you," Rob said, pulling out his pistol and clicking the safety off.

"Let's do this shit then," P said, pulling out his twin .40s.

"You ridin' or what, Chief?" P asked.

"I wouldn't miss this kinda action for nothin'. Let's wet these pigs up."

"Let's do this shit then. It's two of 'em in the car. I'ma hit a couple blocks, then we gon' hop out and let the fireworks begin."

"Let's do this shit and get it over with," Chief said, cocking his nine with the extended clip.

Dre switched lanes a couple of times, putting a couple of cars in between him and the Caprice, and made a quick right turn down a residential street, losing the cops for a minute. He parked, and they all jumped out the truck with their guns aimed in the direction they knew the Caprice would come from. As soon as the Caprice turned onto the street, all four of them unloaded on the car.

The car skidded to a stop, and the cops rolled out of the car and started returning fire. P ran across the street, hid behind a car parked in a driveway, and started firing at the cop on the driver's side of the car. Rob and P had him in a crossfire.

P let off four quick shots: *boom, boom, boom, boom*—and blew the whole top of the cop's head off. As he turned to fire at the other cop, he saw Dre take a direct hit to the face. Blood and brains flew all over the side of Dre's truck. He knew Big Dre was dead.

Rob saw Dre take the bullet to the face at the same time. Rob jumped up from his hiding space in front of the truck and ran directly at the cop who was shooting over the top of the passenger door of the Caprice, screaming, "Not my nigga!"

He was busting shots as he ran towards the cop. Chief and Pecas saw it like it was in slow motion. Rob took three direct hits to the chest but never stopped running towards the cop. He got within five feet of the cop and emptied the rest of the clip into the cop's face.

"Die, muthafucka, die!" he screamed, then started kicking the officer in the face before he collapsed on the side of him.

"Them niggas dead. Let's get the fuck outta here," Chief said.

P noticed several people had come outside to see where all the shooting was coming from. He threw his hood over his head, and he and Chief took off running. They went through alleys, hopped over fences until they came to an apartment complex.

They went into a breezeway and slowed to a walk, breathing hard and trying to catch their breath.

"P, we gotta get the fuck outta this neighborhood before cops shut this bitch down," Chief said.

"I know, man. What the fuck got into Rob? He ran right into those bullets like he was tryin' to get killed," P said.

"That nigga flipped after he seen Dre get killed. He had to have been hit five or six times, but he made sure he smoked that pig before he gave up the ghost."

"He went berserk on that pig," P said, replaying the scene in his mind. "Look at them niggas right there in the parking lot. Let's see if they'll give us a ride outta this area."

Chief looked over to where P was pointing, and they both headed in the direction of the four black guys standing around a box Chevy on 26-inch rims.

"Yo, my nigga, I got twenty-five hundred if you can give me and my nigga a ride outta this neighborhood. We just got into a shootout with the laws a few blocks over," P told them.

"Shit, for twenty-five hundred, I'll take you wherever you wanna go. Get in," the tallest one said, pulling out his car keys.

"Alright, y'all be safe, and fuck the police," one of them said.

Once they were out of the neighborhood, P gave the driver the twenty-five hundred and pulled out his phone and called Omar.

"Bro, the laws just killed Rob and Dre."

"Come on, P, not my niggas. What the fuck happened?"

"They started following us, and we had a shootout with them. It was two of 'em in an unmarked car. The two laws got killed too. Me and Chief took off running. We got a nigga to give us a ride outta the area. We gotta get the fuck outta here for a minute."

"Go to the spot and chill until I can figure out what the fuck to do. You think the laws know who y'all are?"

"I doubt it right now, but you know they gon' try and track their movements down and see who their friends are, so we can't be nowhere around."

"Just go to the spot and lay low. I'm come holla at you later, and y'all niggas stay the fuck off the streets."

"Nuff said, we on it."

Chapter 12

Smurf was at the mall with his daddy Tiger, getting his wardrobe tight after two and a half years in the county jail fighting a murder charge. The charges had been dropped due to lack of evidence, and two nights ago, Smurf opened the front door of the house him and Trina had bought in Garland, and there was Tiger, hair wild as fuck, beating on the door.

"I'm free, Lil' Nigga, put me on," was all Tiger said.

"That's automatic," Smurf said before hugging him and inviting him in. "But first, we gotta do something with yo' wild ass head."

"I need my shit braided, washed, and braided. Where Trina at?"

"She in the kitchen, she pregnant, you finna be a granddaddy."

"Trina," Tiger called out. "Come braid your father-in-law's hair."

A few seconds later, she came waddling in the room with her stomach sticking out.

"Damn, you look like you 'bout to have the baby any day. When you due?"

"In two weeks. Hey, Tiger, I'm glad to see you home and free," she said, giving him a hug.

"Shit, I'm glad to be free. Where your brother at?" he asked Smurf.

"Somewhere in Colorado. I haven't talked to him since the funeral."

"You gotta let that shit go. He fucked up and he know it. That's guilt he gotta live with for the rest of his life. Being mad at him ain't gon' bring Riff back. Y'all brothers, and we family. He just ain't built for the streets. But both of y'all my sons, and we gon' be a family. He put in a little work, he just ain't built like us."

"What you mean he put in some work? That nigga ain't did shit. He just up and left me out here by myself."

"Naw, Lil' Nigga. Yogi the one who smoked Lil' Gutta, and he accidentally killed Dee-Man's little niece when he shot they house up. That's why he left—'cause that little girl got killed. I fuck with the streets, so the streets fuck with me. Don't shit go on out here that I don't know about or can't find out about, ya dig?"

"I didn't even know that shit right there," Smurf admitted.

"Another thing you don't know, your boy Yakki done started smoking that work with his mama."

"Get off that bullshit, daddy. Yakki a G, and he a made nigga. He ain't gon' go out like no sucka."

"Boy, what I just tell you? I am the streets. I don't start rumors or make frivolous talk. Nigga, I'm a triple OG. If I tell you something, take it to the bank and cash that check, it's solid."

So that's why money been coming up short, that nigga been missin' in action a lot too, and the last time I saw him, that nigga's hair wasn't freshly braided like it usually is, Smurf thought to himself. I'ma go by the nigga mama house and see for myself, he planned.

"Smoker's talk, and he been over there tricking with the smokers and fucking the shit out of them. I got word in the county about a week ago."

That was three days ago. Now they were at the mall, and Tiger was tearing the mall up. They had already made two trips to the truck to drop off bags. Next, he was gonna take Tiger to the car lot and buy him a car.

They were in the Gucci store when Smurf's phone went off. He looked at the screen and saw that it was a call from Omar.

"What up?"

"Bro, I need you to get over here as soon as you can."

"What's up? I'm at the mall with Tiger."

"Not on the phone, y'all just get over here ASAP."

"I'm on the way," he said, hanging up the phone. "Daddy, we gotta go. Omar just called and told me to come to the house ASAP."

"What's going on?"

"I don't know. He wouldn't talk on the phone."

"Let's go then," Tiger said, throwing the stack of clothes he had in his arm down.

"Bring that shit on. We can pay for it on the way out the door."

When they got to the house in Cedar Creek, Smurf saw the cars of the whole team parked outside the house.

"Something went down, everybody here," Smurf told Tiger.

"We here now, let's go see what's crackin'," he said as Smurf parked.

Zell answered the door, and Smurf said, "Hey, Zell, this is me and Shayla's dad, Tiger. Dad, this Zell, Omar's wife."

"I know that boy, we met at the funeral."

"Oh, I forgot about that."

Zell hugged both of them and told them, "Everyone's in the entertainment room. Hurry before Shayla hears your voice and comes running. I'll tell her y'all are here so you can see her after the meeting."

"Alright, thanks, Zell," Tiger said.

They went to the entertainment room and saw the whole team sitting around looking angry and somber at the same time.

"Everybody, this is my dad, Tiger," Smurf said.

"Tiger, what up, OG?" Omar said, giving him a hug. Brazy, Slime, D-Money, Bobi, and everyone who knew him already got up and showed him some love.

"It's all good, and I can't thank you enough. That lawyer you got is a bad muthafucka. Thanks, my nigga."

"It's love, OG. You raised us young niggas up in the hood and showed us what that G shit was all about. I wish we were here celebrating your release, but we meetin' today on a sad note."

"What's the deal? Where my nigga Rob at?" Smurf asked.

"Rob and Big Dre got killed yesterday in a shootout with the two federal agents," Omar told him.

"Naw, not my nigga!" Smurf yelled with tears in his eyes.

Lisa got up and hugged him. "Come on, Lil' Bro, hold it together."

"I'm good, Lisa," he said, hugging her back. "Not my nigga though. What happened?"

"The laws were tryin' to question Dre about an undercover agent who disappeared in Nebraska. Big Dre, Rob, P, and Chief were on their way to check out that property for the sports bar when the laws started following them. Them niggas shot it out with two pigs. They killed them, but Dre and Rob got killed also."

"They got P and Chief too?"

"Naw, them niggas in Mexico by now. The laws don't even know who they are. They just left so they could lay low for a while," Omar told him.

"Damn, this shit fucked up."

"Look, y'all," Lisa started, "my nigga was a gangsta and went out like a gangsta. He took two pigs with him. I don't want nobody crying or feeling sorry for Rob . . . he wouldn't want that. We are going to celebrate the time we had with him and carry his legacy on with us. Plus, I'm pregnant, so all y'all niggas is gonna be godfathers to our baby." She said, rubbing her stomach.

"Now that's what a gangsta bitch. Uh, I'm sorry for calling you a—"

Lisa stopped him, "You ain't said shit wrong, OG. I'm a gangsta bitch! Let's pour up and roll up and smoke one for the homies."

They did just that.

Chapter 13

Three days after the death of Robert, MOB Records released the first single from the group The MOB called "When the Lights Go Off." It was a song about being a star in front of the camera, but when the lights go out, are you the same person you claim to be in your songs? Most people thought the song was about dying, and Lisa, being the young genius that she was, did nothing to change people's thinking or try to correct them. The song was an immediate hit.

She got Yolonda, whose sister was an actress and pop star, to sing the chorus. His coffin was pulled down Audelia and Forest Lane by four black horses in a red carriage while the song blasted from speakers hooked to the carriage. Thousands of people lined the streets to pay their respects to MOB Rob. Lisa, in her black dress and veil, rode in the carriage with the other members of MOB, waving to the crowd.

After Robert's funeral, they all drove to Austin, Texas, for Big Dre's service. Em took it the hardest since she had known Dre most of their lives and grew up together.

Two weeks after Big Dre's funeral, Kawanna had to call Omar to go to the South and get George. George had gone on a killing spree.

He was in his hood one night before Dre had been killed and almost got shot up in a war that his hood had going with the Crips from Dixon Circle.

Since Dre's funeral, he had been going out every night and taking his hurt and pain out on their hood. Kawanna had called Omar and asked him to go find George and talk some sense into him before he ended up back in prison or dead.

Omar and Em drove around the South until they found George sitting in his car at the hood store, Little World, in his neighborhood.

"Park right here," he told Em and got out, walking over to get in the passenger seat of George's car.

For a long minute, they just sat there, not saying a word, before George said, "I know you didn't come all the way over here just to sit in the car with me."

"I know you are hurting, my nigga, and I'm hurting too. But I'm also mad as a muthafucka at Dre, 'cause that's that same selfish shit he used to do when we were locked up. But this time it cost him his life. He got blood killed with him, and two more niggas gonna die if the laws ever find out who Chief and Pecas are. I told that nigga to get a lawyer and go talk to them folks, but you know how he is. You can't tell him shit once he make up his mind about something. Kawanna ain't gon' wait on you. No matter how many niggas you kill out here, Big Dre still gon' be gone. You still gon' wake up in the morning feeling the same thing you feel tonight. You gotta find some other kind of way to deal with the pain. You just gon' end up hurting the people that love you more than you are hurting. That woman stayed with you all them years while you were locked up, to spend her life with you. Not to have it end like this—with you dead or back in prison. Go home and let that woman help you deal with that hurt and pain. That's how I got through Lil' Chris' death. Zell helped me deal with it. I loved on her, and it helped me not hate the world. That's what you gotta do. Go home, my nigga, and get out these streets. That girl worried and hurting, not knowing if you coming home or not."

He looked over at George and saw tears falling from his eyes. But he was nodding, yeah. George stuck his hand out, and they locked up.

"I'm finna go home and love on this white woman. I'll check on you in the morning."

"I love you, Bro," George said before Omar got out the car.

"I love you too, Blood."

Omar was shook up over the death of so many of his friends in such a short time. He didn't leave the house for over a month. He stayed in and played with the kids and helped Zell and Shalika with the newborns, since they had both given birth to two boys three days apart, with Shalika being first. Shalika named her son Omarion, and Zell named her son O'Shay. Both boys weighed seven pounds at birth.

Omar changed diapers, warmed bottles, and fed both babies every morning. He started to enjoy the peaceful mornings and the time he had alone with the boys. He would sit in the rocking chair in the nursery with a baby in each arm and rock them back to sleep after feeding them.

Lisa had talked Yolonda into doing an album, so Shalika and Yolonda spent all day at the studio. After the boys were fed and back sleeping, Omar would go back in the bedroom and cuddle with Zell.

One morning, they were laying in bed, and Omar asked her, "Baby, you ever thought about dying?"

"Sometime."

"I wonder where we go when we die?"

"I don't know. If you believe in God, then I guess you go to heaven."

"But what is heaven? It can't be what everybody say it is—a bunch of people sitting up with their old loved ones and family members who died before them."

"How we know that's true if nobody ever died and came back to tell us what was really going on in heaven?"

"We don't, that's the mystery of it. That's why you have to make a decision to trust the word and believe or not trust the word."

"It's crazy we take all these prison chances chasing the money, and then when you get it, you have more problems than before you got it."

"I told you the night we made our relationship official that money couldn't make you happy," Zell reminded him.

"I remember that. But maybe it's us starting off broke and getting caught up in a way of life, and then when we get the money, not knowing how to adapt to a different way of living. You can't keep doing the shit you were doing when you get rich that you were doing when you were broke.

"I know, and sometimes you have to be smart enough to know when you have enough money. Some people get caught up in making the fast money, they don't know when to stop."

"Yeah, that's real talk. Damn, I love you so much," Omar said, hugging her.

"I love you too."

"You know what I want to do?"

"No more babies."

"Naw, not that," he said, smiling. "I wanna build about fifteen more houses on this land so all of my family and friends can be close to me. The way people are dying, I need my people close to me so we can spend as much time as we can together. We can even give your mom a house."

"I will support whatever you want to do. I'm happy seeing you happy."

"Have you noticed that Danielle has a boyfriend?" Zell asked.

"She has a what? Why we haven't met him yet?"

"You have met him. It's Brandon."

"Brandon?"

"Yes, B-Dub."

"Hell naw, you playin', right?"

"No, I'm not playin'. They've been sneaking around since the cruise. Remember the girl Brandon brought?"

"Yeah."

"Danielle made him send her back home. That's why she left early."

"Oh shit, my baby girl put her foot down like that."

"Evidently she did."

"Dub a good guy. How you feel about that?"

"She's nineteen. I'm not going to get in her love life."

"If she happy, I guess I'm cool with it. But, I'm going to let them know they ain't gotta hide from us."

"I think they'll both like that."

"Damn, baby, that ass getting fatter," he said, squeezing her butt.

"I need to hit the treadmill?" she asked.

"Hell no, I love your ass."

"Is that all you love?"

"Naw, I love your titties too. They are huge. I wonder what that milk taste like."

"Ooh, you so nasty," she said, giggling. "Taste it," she said, pulling them out of her gown and putting one in his mouth.

Chapter 14

While Zell and Omar were discussing them, Danielle and B-Dub were at his condo, fucking like two wild animals. Danielle was sitting on Dub's face, riding his tongue like a go-kart.

"Oh shit, I'm about to cum! Lick it faster!" she yelled. "Just like that. Oh yeah, don't stop, keep doing that."

Dub was gone over Danielle. He loved the way she took control of every situation. Like the day they really started dating. They were on the bus on the way to the ship to go on the cruise. He brought a girl he was dating from the hood. When they stopped for gas, Danielle got him alone and said, "Don't bring no bitch around me. I been watching you watching me for the last month. I know you want me. Get rid of that bitch!" she said before walking off.

The next day, the girl was gone, and Danielle ignored him for the next three days.

Zell witnessed everything from the beginning. She told Danielle, "Why are you doing that boy like that?"

"I gotta make sure he really wants me, Mom," she said, smiling.

"He got rid of his girlfriend for you."

"He might just want some new pussy. Men will do almost anything for some new pussy. You know that, Mom."

"Who's been teaching you all of this?"

"My dad, Omar," she said and walked off. Zell just shook her head and smiled.

Now, she was on top of Dub's face, about to cum. "I'm finna cum," she moaned, grinding on his face.

Dub was in a zone, working magic with his tongue while staring up at the expressions Danielle was making. Her eyes were closed, her mouth was slightly open, and she had a look of pure ecstasy on her face.

"Oh shit, I'm cumming," she moaned, her whole body shaking.

"Damn, that was good," she said after a few minutes, rolling off his face and laying next to him.

He cuddled up behind her and easily slid into her warm wetness. "Damn, this pussy good," Dub whispered.

"Don't cum inside me," she said, getting into it, looking over her shoulder and throwing it back.

"I won't, baby," he answered, hitting her with a couple of hard, deep strokes.

"Hit it like that, fuck me hard. Oh shit, I'm about to cum again."

Later, after they were both satisfied, Danielle said, "We have to tell him."

"Tell who what?"

"We have to tell my dad, Omar."

"You think he's gonna be mad?"

"I'm not sure, but I doubt it."

"He might not ever talk to me again."

"Why do you say that? You're his best friend."

"That don't mean shit when it comes to family. He don't want his best friend fucking his daughter."

"So that's all we're doing, is fucking?"

"What do you want us to do, Dan Dan?"

She loved it when he called her Dan Dan. "I don't know, you can't think of anything?"

She was in love with Dub and would marry him if he asked. But she wasn't going to be the one to suggest it. If it wasn't already on his mind, then she wasn't going to make him feel like he had to do it because she wanted him to. She wanted him to do it because he felt the same way about her that she felt about him.

Dub was already on some grown-man shit and knew that he wanted Danielle in his life. But he didn't know how Omar would feel about them, and he was reluctant to approach him about the situation. He knew one day they would eventually have to tell him, or he would find out by some other means, and Dub didn't want that. He wanted to be the one to tell him. He decided that he would just have to man up and tell him and deal with the decision he made concerning his daughter. He knew how Omar felt about Danielle, and he needed him to know that he felt the same way about her and would never intentionally hurt her.

He looked over at Danielle and said, "Let's get engaged."

"Well, that's not exactly the way I envisioned getting proposed to," she said with a slight smile on her face. "But if you are really wanting to do this, I'm down. But you gotta step your game up, I need an extravagant and lavish proposal with a ring," she said, smiling.

"I got you, just wait and see. Let's go talk to your mom and dad."

"Uh oh, you in trouble," she said, laughing.

Chapter 15

Smurf and Tiger had took over the hood. They doubled the package that Smurf was getting from Glenn, and Tiger was moving drugs all over the city.

He had remodeled the house that Red Tina got killed in and moved in so he could be on the block and direct operations without all the chaos. He stood at the window watching the transaction and said to Smurf, "Look how this bitch rollin' when you got good product and no drama around to interrupt a nigga from gettin' money. We done went through at least three bricks on the bust down, and I know we done sold at least ten more whole bricks to these dope boys, niggas. If shit keep goin' like this, I'll be out the game before the year is over with."

"I see this bitch rollin'. It was doin' numbers before all the bullshit started happenin', but Yogi and Riff didn't have the kinda connect we got now."

"Yeah, your boy Omar is plugged in for real. I watched that lil' nigga grow up and knew he was gonna be a certified hustler. That nigga mama, Faye, was a damn fool in the game."

"Daddy, let's go by and see what that nigga Yaki up to. That nigga ain't been on the block in weeks, plus, that nigga still owe me two hundred stacks."

"Man, that nigga smoked out. I know that's your day one nigga, but sometimes you outgrow niggas and you gotta be wise enough to know when to move on and when not to, ya dig?"

"I feel you. But I still gotta look this nigga in the eyes and see for myself. I already know it's true, but I still gotta see it."

"Let's ride then," Tiger said, getting up and heading for the door. After they were in the truck and on their way, Tiger told Smurf, "I like that shit you did."

"What?" Smurf asked.

"That loyalty you showing yo' day one nigga. Never let nobody tell you shit about your niggas that you don't investigate before you make a decision on it. That's real shit right there."

They made it over to the house, parked, and got out. Smurf knocked on the door, and Mrs. Betty opened it a few minutes later.

"Hey, Smurf. Tiger. I'm glad you out. I heard they dropped the charges on you about a week ago."

"Yeah, you know how they do a nigga from the hood. Hold a nigga, knowing they ain't got shit on him, hoping he get weak and cop out or tell on somebody else. Where Yaki at?" he asked after she had let them in and closed the door.

Betty was a tall, dark-complexioned woman that Tiger grew up with in the hood. They were around the same age and went to school together. She used to be one of the baddest chicks in school before Yaki's daddy had turned her onto crack. She was still slightly attractive, but years of smoking, not eating right, and not getting enough sleep had taken its toll on her. You could see the results on her face.

"He back in his room," she said, letting them go down the hallway to his room. She knew why they were there; the streets talk. She had tried warning Yaki about taking a hit or two every now and then, thinking that he could control it, but he wouldn't listen. Now he had a full-grown gorilla on his back.

Smurf could smell the crack smoke coming from the closed door of Yaki's room before he even opened the door. Smurf opened the door without knocking, and they went in.

Yaki was in the middle of the bed with the crack pipe in his mouth and his dick in Cassie's mouth. He looked up and saw Smurf and Tiger and blew out a cloud of smoke across the room.

Cassie was a Mexican chick they went to school with. She was the prettiest Mexican in the hood, and Yaki and her had been fucking around since they were in middle school.

"Hold up, Cassie, my nigga 'nem here," Yaki said, reaching over and putting on his boxers.

"Cuz, you trippin'," Smurf said, looking at him and shaking his head. "All the years we watched how that shit took Mrs. Betty down, and you still took the ride, cuz, you fucked up."

"I know, my nigga. But I'ma get myself back right in a minute. Cuz, I had so much shit on my mind, stressin' and shit, and I fucked up."

"I know you ain't got Cassie in here smokin' that shit too?" Smurf asked.

"Hell naw, she ain't fucking with it."

"Cassie, how you let my nigga go out like that?"

"Smurf, we broke up for a month, and I started hearing rumors on the streets that he was smoking and fucking with these crack hos. So I came by to check on him and found him in here smoked out with two or three of those nasty-ass bitches in here with him. So I ran they ass off, and I been here with him ever since. I just can't get him to stop smoking that shit."

"Cuz, where that bread at? I know you ain't fucked off my money?"

"Hell naw, cuz, I got that bread. Cassie, get that money for him outta the safe."

Cassie got out of the bed in nothing but a pair of panties and a bra and went to the closet.

"And Cassie, put some clothes on while you in there," Smurf said, trying not to look at her ass jiggling as she walked across the room.

She came back out of the closet in a pair of shorts and a t-shirt with a duffle bag and handed it to Smurf. Tiger was just leaning up against the wall, listening.

Smurf looked in the bag, did a quick count, and saw the money was straight. He looked over at Yaki and told him, "I'm disappointed in you, cuz. You gotta get back on point. We getting this money and trying to get out the hood, away from all this shit, and you start smoking just when we about to get right."

"I know, cuz. I'ma get off this shit and be back on the block in a minute," Yaki said.

"I need you here with me, cuz, and you trippin'. You gotta get serious about getting off that shit and bounce back. You know what, as a matter of fact? Get yo' ass up, go take a shower, and get dressed."

"Where we goin'?"

"Just get cleaned up and dressed. I can't leave you here like this. I'm taking yo' ass to rehab right now, or I'ma walk out this door, and you gon' be dead to me, my nigga."

Yaki looked at Smurf for a minute, saw the sincerity in his eyes, and slowly got up and went to take a shower.

"Cassie, get him some clothes to put on," Smurf said.

"Thank you, Smurf," Cassie said, giving him a hug after Yaki had left outta the room to go shower. "You saved my man."

"He ain't saved yet, Cassie. He gotta want this shit, and if he don't, this shit ain't gonna mean nothing. He gon' come right back out here to it. The fight just started."

"He gon' get right. I feel it. He saw how disappointed you are in him."

"I hope so."

Tiger, standing across the room, had his respect for his son raised in the last hour. He liked the way Smurf handled the situation with his nigga and thought, *This nigga really an OG.*

While Yaki was in the shower, Smurf was on his phone, looking up rehabilitation centers in the city. He found a small one in the Turtle Creek area and made the call. He picked that one because it was in the rich part of town, and he didn't want Yaki in the hood or any area where it would be easy for him to get drugs if he fell off the wagon.

He talked to a lady on the phone and explained the situation. She took down Yaki's information and told Smurf to bring him over. It was a 90-day program, and he wouldn't be able to have a cell phone or leave until the last month. He would be able to leave for four hours on the weekends with family. After he hung up the phone, he told Cassie to pack him some clothes.

"Thank you, Smurf, for loving Yaki just as much as I do," she said, giving him a hug with tears in her eyes.

"That's my nigga, you ain't gotta thank me, we family."

Yaki got the shower, got dressed, hugged and kissed his mom, then they all went out, got in the truck, and drove out to the rehab.

Yaki was quiet on the drive to the rehab. Him and Cassie sat in the back, holding hands and whispering. Tiger was getting calls on his phone from niggas trying to get bricks and half bricks. Smurf was in his own world, hoping that in 90 days, Yaki would be back to his old self so they could get back to getting money.

The building was a two-story brick building on the corner of the street. When they got to the reception desk, Smurf told the lady that they had just talked to someone on the phone and that his friend was trying to get in the program. She told them to have a seat in the waiting area while she got one of the counselors.

A few minutes later, a tall, middle-aged white woman came out and took them to her office, where she explained how the program worked, what Yaki could and couldn't do. She had Yaki sign a bunch of papers. She asked if Yaki had insurance, and Smurf told her that he was paying for it. She explained the cost and the payment methods. Since Smurf or Tiger didn't have a credit card, he had to call Omar to get him to pay with his credit card, and he would bring the cash over to him.

Once everything was paid for and all the paperwork was filled out, she gave them 30 minutes with Yaki to say their goodbyes. Smurf hugged him, and Tiger shook his hand.

"Bro, we gon' go outside and let you and Cassie have some time alone. I'll be back every weekend to visit."

"Alright, cuz, I appreciate this, my nigga."

"It's all love, cuz," Smurf told him, and they walked outside.

"You think he gonna make it?" Smurf asked Tiger after they got outside.

"I hope he do. He got a lot of support. I hope he get his shit together," Tiger said, but in the back of his mind, he was thinking that Yaki was just like his mama—a dope fiend.

Chapter 16

Omar was back in Florida with his family, his mom, and Pops. He had decided to build fifteen more houses on his property, and construction workers were all over the place, so they went back to Florida.

The money was still rolling from his legal businesses and from his side hustle. Glenn was still pushing the work off to D-Money and Bobi. Smurf, Tiger, and Omar had talked Bobi and D-Money into letting Slime take over the Lane. So Slime was doing his thing and making a killing on the Lane.

Omar and Slime had gotten real close. Slime was business-minded, and Omar wanted to help him get out the game and get into some legal shit.

Slime had already invested some of his money into three paint and body shops. Omar, Dub, and Slime had also bought ten 18-wheeler trucks and were in the process of opening a trucking company.

Slime already had it set in his mind that he would be out the game and completely legal in the next year or year and a half.

Omar looked out his bedroom window and saw Danielle and Dub laying on towels in the sand by the ocean. He thought back to the day Dub and Danielle finally came and told him about their relationship.

He was upstairs playing with the kids when his phone beeped, letting him know he had a message. He looked at the phone and saw that the message was from Zell. He opened the message and read, "Can you come down to the family room? Danielle wants to talk to you."

He told the kids he would be back later and went downstairs. When he got to the family room, Zell, Shalika, Danielle, and Dub were sitting around looking nervous.

"What's up, y'all?"

"They want to tell you something," Zell said, pointing at Dub and Danielle.

"What's up, baby girl? Y'all alright?"

Danielle nodded her head yes, and Dub said, "Big Bro, I don't even know how to tell you this, but me and Dee have been seeing each other."

"Y'all see each other every day. Shit, you here almost every day. What's wrong with that?" Omar said, playing dumb. He already knew what they wanted to talk about. Ever since Zell had told him about their relationship, he was just waiting on them to come tell him.

"It's a little more complicated than that," Shalika said.

"Man, what the hell are y'all talking about?" Omar asked impatiently.

"Uh, me and Danielle want to, uh, get married, and we wanted to know if it was okay with you?" Dub finally said.

For a long while, Omar just sat there staring from Dub to Danielle. Finally, he looked at Danielle and said, "Danielle, are you pregnant?"

"No," she answered, shaking her head.

"How long has this been going on between you two?"

"Since the cruise," Danielle answered.

"Since the cruise? That was almost two years ago. Y'all been sneaking around since the cruise?"

Danielle nodded yes, while staring at the floor.

"Shalika, did you know about this?"

"Everybody knew except you, I guess," Shalika answered.

"Yolonda, did you know?"

"No," Yolonda said.

"So, Zell, you knew?"

"Yes."

"So almost everybody in the house knew except me. So that's what we're doing in this house now? Keeping secrets? Let's get something understood right now between all of us. Family don't keep secrets from each other. No more secrets in this house. If something is going on in this house, especially with my kids, I need to know immediately." Omar turned to Danielle and Dub and said, "Now, when do y'all plan on getting married?"

"Uh, we haven't set a date yet. We wanted to see if it was okay with you first," Danielle said.

"Y'all let me know when you set a date," Omar said, getting up and leaving them in the room.

He smiled thinking back to that day. He stood at the window a little longer, watching them before he finally left the window.

He went downstairs and got ready to drive Shalika and Yolonda to the airport so they could go back to Dallas. Lisa had Yolonda in the studio recording her first album. She had already sung backup on her sister's album. So now she was recording her own music, and her sister, Sharonda, was going to record several songs with her.

He put their bags in the truck, and they got in the truck with Em driving. They headed for the airport.

Omar sat in the back with Shalika and Yolonda, whispering in each other's ears, talking freaky, telling each other what they were going to do to each other when they came back.

Before long, Yolonda and Shalika were giving him head, and he was fingering them. "Oh shit, I gotta get me some of this dick," Shalika said, pulling her pants down and sitting on Omar's lap. She rode him until she had an orgasm. She climbed off him and sucked her juices off his dick.

"Come on, Yolonda, you better hurry up, we almost at the airport." Yolonda hurried and removed her pants and rode

75

him all the way to the airport. She sucked her juices off him, fixed their clothes, and hurried into the airport.

They checked their luggage in and sat around waiting until it was time for their departure. When it was time for them to board the plane, Omar walked them to the gate, hugged, and squeezed both their asses, and they left.

When they got back in the truck, Em looked at Omar and said, "That shit got my pussy leaking watching y'all. Can you put this fire out for me?" she asked, smiling.

"You know I wasn't going back to the house without getting some of that good-ass pussy. Find a quiet place to park so I can fuck the shit outta you."

Em drove around until she found a motel that was almost empty and sat back off the street. She pulled in and parked, then climbed in the back seat with Omar, where he beat her back in.

Chapter 17

Slime was at the spot with his workers. It was only mid-afternoon, and they had already reupped three times and made over three hundred thousand dollars. Ever since Bobi and D-Money had turned the Lane over to Slime, he had increased their intake in revenue.

He made sure all his workers were money-motivated and not on any messy-ass, dry beefing-with-niggas shit. He had six spots trolling on and around the Lane, and all of them were making tons of money. He even had a spot where the smokers could come chill and get high. Some of the smokers, who had been up for two or three days chasing that paper, he made them go to the spot, take a shower, and get some sleep. On weekends, they barbecued, and all the smokers were offered free plates. He made sure his workers respected the smokers, and the smokers loved and respected him for the way he treated them. They loved spending their money with him and at his spots.

Slime stayed on the phone with Omar, picking his brain about investing and how to double up his money. He knew the game didn't last forever, and he wanted to exit the game on his own terms, just like his big homie Omar, and not let law enforcement dictate when he left the game.

He started out at the strip clubs and kept his stuntin' to a minimum. He was a young nigga and loved to floss for the bitches, but he kept it to a level that wouldn't attract the attention of the FEDS.

The jackboys in the hood already knew how they put it down on some gangsta shit, so they never tried to rob any of his spots. He was quietly getting money and moving product. The cartel, Ole Man Santos, was taking notice and letting Omar know that Slime was doing a good job. Slime started to notice that his packages were increasing and he was getting more product to sell.

Bobi and D-Money were running the operation, but Slime was the breadwinner and the money getter. Everyone was taking notice of Slime's hard work, so much so that Omar had finally talked Glenn into giving Slime the game on how to cook the dope up and cut it.

Glenn was reluctant to do it because that was his game. Niggas all over the city paid Glenn to cook their work up for them. So Glenn didn't like the idea of giving another nigga the game to take food off his plate. But Omar had to remind Glenn that he was outta the game and that Slime was on their team. Finally, after weeks of talking, he convinced Glenn to give Slime the cook-up game.

Slime spent two weeks at the condo with Glenn learning how to rock up the dope. Glenn showed him the basics, then he cooked up four ounces while Slime watched. Then he put it back in the microwave and melted it down again, telling Slime to try it.

The first couple of times he tried it, he couldn't get the dope to rock up into a solid block. But after doing it several times, he started to get the hang of it, and the dope started to come back right.

Glenn had six microwaves scattered around the kitchen, and before the two weeks were up, Slime was running all six of them at the same time. He cooked up ten bricks so fast that Glenn gave him an extra key to the condo and told him he had free access to the condo to cook his shit whenever he needed to. Slime knew that Omar and the fam were fucking with him the long way. He went back to the Lane with determination and a newfound zest to run up some numbers.

"Blood, it's new niggas poppin' up all over the hood. These niggas setting up spots in our territory, and a couple of them getting a little money," Lil Mob was telling Slime.

"When Short Dogg 'nem was on the block, we would've been done ran them niggas off," Lil Mob continued.

"That was a different time," Slime informed him. "Back then, they were trying to establish the hood. Them niggas put in so much work around the hood that niggas know how we get down. We ain't gotta do that shit no more. Shooting niggas brings the laws around, and when the laws come around, a nigga can't make no money. Them niggas can't go rock for rock or brick for brick with us. We got an unlimited supply, so all we gotta do is make our shit bigger and stronger, then we'll starve them niggas out. Eventually, they'll relocate after they see they can't get no money."

Slime was up on all the hood politics, and he knew that Lil Mob was referring to a nigga named Kenyatta. He was the only nigga in the hood that wasn't on their team, getting any money.

But Slime had already gotten the background on Kenyatta. Yatta grew up in the hood and went to school with Short Dogg. When he started hustling, he went to the South with his uncles and built his clientele. His people were plugged in, and they made a lot of money. The FEDS had hit the uncle and got him on a conspiracy charge to distribute a hundred pounds or more of marijuana. He took a three-year sentence, and Kenyatta moved back to the hood. But he brought all his customers with him. He didn't sell dope to random niggas. Everybody that scored from him were niggas he had been fucking with in the South.

Yatta had a good connect, and he had some quality dope, so it didn't make a difference what area he was in—he was going to get off his product. Plus, he was well-respected all over the city for doing good business and being a stand-up nigga.

But what nobody knew was that Rudy was Kenyatta's connect, and Rudy, being on some ho shit, had been talking to Yatta about how the old hood was jumping and encouraged Yatta to move back on the Lane until his uncle came back home, hoping that Yatta would get into it with the MOB.

Chapter 18

It was Saturday night, and everybody was at the Red Door #2 celebrating the return of Yakki. Smurf and Cassie had picked Yakki up Friday morning from rehab.

Yakki had completed the program and came out of rehab looking like his old self. He had gained his weight back and buffed up from working out in the gym while he was there.

"You lookin' good, my nigga," Smurf told him once he'd gotten through hugging and kissing Cassie.

"I feel good, my nigga. I told you I was gonna get back on my shit. I'm ready to get this bag for real now. It's crunch time, we in the fourth quarter, with the game on the line. I'm 'bout to hit the block hard for the next 12 months, and then I'm through with the game and the streets. I'ma marry my bitch and get somewhere and sit down."

"What the fuck I done told you about calling me your bitch, asshole?" Cassie said, correcting him. "I'm your woman!"

"That's my fault, baby. But, you know I'm a hood nigga, and when I call you my bitch, I mean you are beautiful, intelligent, terrific, charismatic, and hypnotic. So stop all that lame shit, you know how I feel about you. Without you, there ain't no me. You are my future, so don't ever think I'm belittling you or disrespecting you when I call you my bitch." Yakki laid his game down on the only girlfriend that he'd ever had or wanted.

Cassie was blushing. She leaned over and gave Yakki a wet kiss. "I know, baby. I'm sorry for acting like a lame."

"Bro, I got you a suite for a month at the W hotel, and look in that bag back there on the floor, that's yours."

"What's this?" Yakki asked after he'd opened the bag and saw that it was full of money.

"Nigga, that's 1.5 million right there," Smurf told him.

"Damn, my nigga, you been getting the money. But what's this for?" Yakki asked.

"Nigga, that's your half of the money from the spot. I know you didn't think I wasn't gonna hold it down for my day one, did you?"

"Damn, my nigga, that's some real shit right there. I don't even deserve this 'cause I know I fucked up and let you down, fam. But I'm back on my grind," Yakki said, trying not to get emotional.

"Stop actin' like a lame, my nigga. The same thing you just told Cassie. We started this shit together. No matter what, I'ma hold it down for us the same way I'd expect you to hold it down if I had to be gone for a minute," Smurf told him.

"I love you, my nigga, and I appreciate this."

"It's all love, bro, and that ain't shit. Watch what we finna do."

That was Friday. Now they sat in the private club at the Red Door #2 on the second floor. Cassie was looking like a baby back rib in a skirt. Her ass was so fat that every time she moved, it looked like her ass was talking.

Smurf and Trina came in looking like the perfect couple. Trina had gotten thicker in all the right places since she'd had the baby. With her dark skin and highlights in her hair, she was looking like a thicker Kelly Rowland.

Lisa was hosting the party with Junior and Brazy. She had the baby about six months ago and had immediately gotten in the gym and got her body back right. She was already a bad bitch with her light complexion and hazel green eyes. The baby had also made her titties and ass fatter.

Omar came in with his whole family, including his mom Faye, his pops, his sister Connie, Zell, Shalika, Yolonda, Em, K-Rock, J-Low, and Yolonda's sister Sharonda and her boyfriend Todd.

Connie had the biggest ass in the building by far. With Shalika, Mama Faye, and Yolonda coming in second, third, and fourth. Connie's ass was so fat it looked like she needed an extra pair of legs to help her carry it. She knew exactly what to wear to show off her ass. She had on a long dress that hugged her hips and ass.

Shalika, being the amazon she was, came in wearing designer blue jean shorts that hugged her voluptuous ass, high heels, and a top that showed off her flat stomach.

Faye had on white see-through pants and a top with black panties and a bra. Her ass was so big it looked like she was mixed with a mule.

"Pops, why you let Mama come out here in that?" Omar asked after he had hugged and kissed his mom on the cheek.

"I had to let these young niggas see what a real woman look like," Pops said, enjoying the fact that he had one of the baddest chicks in the house.

"What you talking about, boy? What's wrong with my clothes?" Faye asked.

"Mama, I can see your panties, and them pants too tight. How long did it take you to get them on?" Omar said, teasing his mom.

"Wait 'til I get a couple drinks in me, I'mma hit the dance floor and show these young bitches how to make this ass clap," Faye said, swinging her hips to the music.

"If you do that, I'ma make security put you out too," Omar told her.

"Boy, boo, my children own this club. I'll make an OG call, and yo' ass might get put out tonight," Faye said, laughing.

"I'm one of the owners," he reminded her.

"Yeah, I know. But my baby boy is one of the owners and managers, and my oldest is the chef and the owner, so you overruled," Faye said, enjoying the moment.

Just as she got through talking, Junior, Glenn, Dell, and Jay walked up.

"Damn, Mama, you killing them pants. You look good," Junior said.

"Now!" she said, turning to Junior, giving her other boys a hug and a kiss.

"Junior, you can see through them clothes," Omar said.

"Let me see." Just as Faye was spinning around to let her boys check out her outfit, Connie walked up and slapped Faye on the ass.

"Oh, Mama, you look good," Connie said.

"Thank you, baby," Faye answered.

"Excuse me, Lil' Mama," Dell said to Faye, "can I have this dance?" he asked, taking her hand.

"Of course, you can," she said, giving Connie her purse before sashaying out to the dance floor with Dell.

They all stood there watching them walk to the dance floor. Omar turned to Pops and told him, "Pops, if that wasn't my Mama, I'd pull her from you."

"Little nigga, stop with the nonsense, that's on lock," Pops assured him.

"Pops, yo' game ain't like that?" Omar said.

"It sure ain't," Glenn added.

Pops just looked at them for a few seconds before he said, "Nigga, my game tighter than a bumblebee's pussy, and when you got the dick game to match it, it's shut down!"

They all burst out laughing.

Just then, Zell, Shalika, and Yolonda walked up. "Hey, y'all," Zell greeted them. "Where Mama Faye?"

"Out there on the dance floor with Dell," Omar told them and nodded.

"Damn, Mama Faye look hot!" Shalika said. "Come on, Yolonda."

Shalika said, grabbing Yolonda's hand, heading to the dance floor to dance with Faye and Dell.

"She does look good," Zell admitted.

"I know, she look too good. I don't want to have to kill nobody over my mama," Omar said, laughing.

"You look good too, baby," Omar whispered in Zell's ear while squeezing her ass.

"Thank you, baby. Do I look good enough to eat?" she asked, whispering in his ear.

"You know you do," he answered.

"Don't talk about it, be about it. Come on then," she said, grabbing his hand and leading him to the private office.

Chapter 19

As the party went on, everyone was having a good time enjoying themselves. The waiters came in and served steaks, seafood, oxtails, salads, and every kind of food you could think of. Wine and drinks were served before Yakki got up and took the floor to speak.

"Excuse me, y'all, let me say a few words before we get back to the party. First of all, I want to thank my brother from another mother for always having my back and making sure I stay on point. Smurf, thank you, my nigga. Second, I want to say that my mom couldn't be here tonight 'cause she's in rehab trying to get herself right. I need y'all to keep her in your prayers. Third, I want to thank my girlfriend since sixth grade. Cassie, come up here. This woman right here is the love of my life, and I want to thank you for always having my back and being there for me, even through all the bullshit I've put you through. Sometimes a nigga needs some time alone without all the distractions to re-evaluate everything and realize what's important to him. You are the most important person in my life, and I want to ask you something tonight in front of all our friends and family." He reached into his pocket and handed Cassie a small gift-wrapped box. While she was opening it, he dropped to one knee and took her hand. "Will you marry me?"

He took the ring out of the box and put it on her finger. Cassie was speechless. "Are you serious?" she asked.

Just then, her mother and father walked up and stood beside them. She knew then that he was serious and that this had all been planned. Her mother was smiling, tears coming out of her eyes. Cassie started crying, seeing how happy her mother was for her.

"Hell yeah, I'll marry you," she said, throwing herself into his arms and giving him a sloppy, wet kiss.

As soon as she said yes, the whole club started clapping and shouting. Then the DJ played "Let's Get Married" by Jagged Edge. The waitresses came out with bottles of champagne, and the party was on.

Chapter 20

Yakki was back to his old self. He had been out of rehab for six months and was back on his grind hard. He had a month and a half before he was to marry Cassie. He was trying to get his money right without dipping into his stash. He wanted to do it big for his wedding and honeymoon.

With OG Tiger coming home and getting back in the game, Smurf and Yakki had to split the money coming off the block with Tiger. Tiger owned the house they were selling the work out of, so he automatically had to get in on the money.

Smurf and Yakki agreed to split up and get their own little crew together and put the lil' niggas in a spot. They would still work the block together, but they would have their own little side hustle going.

Yakki had a little cousin who was nineteen. Everyone called him Baby Boy. He was a lil' nigga, only about five foot two and a buck thirty at the most. But he was one of the most feared niggas in the hood and he was straight crippin'. He was 357 Grave Yard Gangsta Crip.

Baby Boy was hustling, but he was clock hustling. A nigga can't get nothing but some outfit money standing on the block. Yakki knew Baby Boy was about his money, so he was going to put the nigga in the spot and let him get at some real money.

Yakki drove to the south in his smoke-gray Navigator on 28s. The inside of the truck had been completely redone in wood grain and Gucci interior, including the seats. It had 18s and a forty-thousand-dollar sound system.

Before he even made it to his aunt's house, he drove by the hood store, and just like he figured, Baby Boy was there with three other lil' niggas. All had some form of blue clothing on. They were all leaning up against the front of the store, passing a blunt. Yakki pulled up in front of them and parked. A couple of the lil' niggas started reaching for their waists when Baby Boy told them, "He good, that's my cuzzin."

Yakki rolled down the window and said, "Come ride with me for a minute, cuz."

"Y'all hold the block down for a minute. Let me holla at my fam." Baby Boy got in the passenger seat, and Yakki drove off.

"What's crackin', cuz?" Baby Boy asked.

"Cuz, you know me. It's all about a dollar with me. Look, I'm tryna put you on some real bread. That block bleedin' ain't gonna get you shit but some outfit money and a beat-up-ass old ride like that reject-ass Malibu you got—"

"Nigga, my shit—" Baby Boy started to get heated.

"Chill, nigga, and listen! I got this spot. I'm tryna put you in and let you run that bitch. We gonna sell weight, from fifties on up to bricks. I got the hook-up on the dro', Gorilla Piss, powder, crack, pills, and drank."

"Where the spot at?" Baby Boy asked.

"It's in the Nawf. I'm finna take you to the spot right now and let you see the setup. Now shut the fuck up and let me jam my shit," Yakki said, turning the music up.

"Fuck you, nigga."

He got to the Trace Townhomes, and Baby Boy saw how nice and quiet it was.

"Man, it's dead over here. A nigga can't get no money, ain't nobody even outside." Baby Boy was heated.

"Just come on, nigga, and stop always talking when you need to be listening," Yakki said, parking the car and getting out.

"Follow me, lil' nigga," Yakki said, leading him to the bottom apartment he had parked in front of.

He unlocked the door and let Baby Boy look around. When you walked in, you were in the living room. Then a huge kitchen, and down a hallway was a bathroom and then the master bedroom. The bedroom was huge with its own bathroom.

To the right of the front door was a set of stairs that led up to the loft with its own bathroom. It also had upstairs and downstairs patios. Baby Boy immediately fell in love with the townhome.

"I like this setup, but we gon' get some money, and ain't nobody outside. Who we gon' sell to?"

"Nigga, you ain't got no customers on your phone?" Yakki asked.

"Yeah, my shit be jumpin' off the hook," Baby Boy bragged.

"Well, start telling them to meet you out here at the spot, and they gonna come. I got a bunch of stripper bitches I'ma be sending y'all way to score."

"I'm down with it, but I gotta have my niggas with me," Baby Boy said.

"Who are your niggas?"

"Them three niggas I was with at the store."

"What's up with them niggas? Are they solid?"

"Yeah, nigga, that's my crew."

"Let's go meet them niggas then."

They pulled back up, and them niggas got in the back of the truck. Yakki pulled back off, pushed a button on the door panel, and a tray slid out the dashboard with about thirty neatly rolled blunts in it. He grabbed three of them and put them in rotation.

"My cuzz got a spot in the North. He wants us to run. It ain't like over here in the hood. We gon' be chillin' in a spot and people gon' come knock on the door. This is a badass spot we gon' be livin' in too," Yakki explained to his niggas.

"Oh yeah, cuz, this nigga behind you is Lil' J. Matter of fact, cuz, this is our cousin. That's Nita's son."

Yakki looked in the rearview mirror, and they locked eyes. They both started smiling at the same time.

"J, what up, cuz? I ain't seen you since y'all moved to Shreveport or some shit when we was little."

"Hell yeah, we went to Shreveport . . ."

"How long you been back?"

"I been back almost four years now."

"So," Baby Boy said, breaking up the family reunion, "you know cuz. This nigga," he said, pointing to the short, stocky nigga with dreads in the middle, "is Lil' Knocky, and the other nigga is Buckwheat." He pointed to a tall, brown-skinned nigga.

"Y'all, this is my cuzzin, Yakki."

"Where they spot at?" Buckwheat asked.

"In the Nawf, nigga, I already said that."

"Nigga, the Nawf is big as fuck. What part of the Nawf?"

"We on our way to the spot right now, so chill and be still and let 'cuz turn up the music."

They went back to the spot and showed them the place. They all liked the setup and agreed.

"So how we gon' do the money?" Buckwheat asked.

"Sixty-forty split," Yakki said.

"Naw, cuz, that ain't no player deal on our part," Buckwheat said.

"Man, you always trippin', Buckwheat," Baby Boy said.

"Dig this, cuz. If we give him sixty-forty, we gotta split that forty percent between us four. That ain't no bread."

They all thought about it for a minute and knew Buckwheat was right. "Fifty-fifty, cuz. That will let us eat too," Baby Boy said.

"Alright, fifty-fifty."

Chapter 21

Over the next couple of days, Yakki was busy getting furniture and other household items they would need. He made sure he got the Xbox and PlayStation and all the latest games.

After they had been settled in for about a week, Yakki went and got the X-Factor, his white girl Brandi.

Brandi and Yakki had been friends for years. Brandi moved in the hood with her family right after she had graduated high school. Yakki and her had fucked around for a little while, but Brandi started smoking crack. But they had always remained cool, and Brandi was a master at getting a spot rolling. She had already worked her magic several times before.

Yakki kept Brandi hid in a two-bedroom condo that he paid for, for her. Brandi was a bad white girl. She was tall and thick, not fat, just thick like a black man would want a white girl. She had a pretty face, green eyes, and long brown hair.

He picked Brandi up from her condo and drove her over to the spot where Baby Boy and his crew were.

"I need you to get this spot jumping for me," he told her on the way to the spot.

They got to the spot and went to the door. Yakki knocked, and they stood waiting for someone to open the door.

Baby Boy answered the door. "What's up, cuz?" he said, opening the door so they could come in.

"Ain't shit," Yakki said as they walked in, and he saw the rest of the crew in front of the Xbox. "This my homegirl Brandi, she gon' come stay with y'all for a few weeks. She gon' get this bitch rolling for us."

They were all four eyeing Brandi with thoughts in their hands about fucking the shit out of her.

"How she gon' get the spot rolling?"

Yakki answered, "In two weeks, this bitch gon' be rolling harder than a bitch."

"Yeah, if you say so," Buckwheat said skeptically.

Yakki didn't even waste his time responding. He took Brandi around and showed her the apartment. Then he took her back to her condo so she could pack and drive her own car out there. Yakki left to go conduct other business.

Later that night, Brandi returned with a few sets of clothes and her hygiene bag. "Y'all need to clean this place up," she told them.

"Don't start all that nagging and shit. Whatever ain't clean enough for you, clean it and leave us the fuck alone," Baby Boy said.

"Well, fuck y'all too," she said, walking out the door.

Brandi walked the streets of the neighborhood. Before she could even get out of one car, another car was picking her up. All potential customers she took to the spot and had them spend some money.

Every night for the next two weeks, Brandi was out walking the streets and bringing new people to the spot to score. With the customers they brought with them, the ones that Yakki had hooked them up with, and the ones Brandi had brought in, the spot was jumping in no time.

They were running through a whole brick a day on the bust down. Not even counting what they did on the weight. They had a one-stop shop going. You could pull up and get any kind of drug you wanted. The money was pouring in, and they were eating like they never had before.

While Yakki was getting his crew together, Smurf and Tiger were making their own connections. They had hooked up with some Five-Deuce Crips outta Fort Worth that he was fronting work to, and they had a spot that was booming on the powder, hard, and heroin.

In the few weeks that they had been working together, them niggas had already moved over five bricks of work all on the bust down. They were some young niggas, but they were straight about getting the bag.

Smurf was putting his money up and investing it in real estate, sports bars, motels, car washes, and buying homes and remodeling them. He was stacking his bread, thinking about his family and his future.

He knew he didn't want to be selling drugs when he got older. He had already made a promise to his wife that he would get out the game within the next three years. So, he was fully focused on getting his brand right.

He laid in the bed next to Trina, who was still asleep, thinking about his plans for the day. He remembered that they were supposed to go out to Omar's house. The construction workers were through, and Omar and his family had moved back in. So, they were all going out there to see the results.

Just as he was about to get out of bed, Trina rolled over and threw her leg over him. Her nightgown was twisted around her, and one of her breasts had fell out. He put his tongue on one of her nipples and felt it immediately harden. She let out a soft moan that sent Smurf over the edge. He started licking and sucking all over her breasts. He almost managed to get one of her whole breasts in his mouth, but it was a little too big. So, he continued to lick and suck on the nipple.

Before long, he had her legs in the air, and he was eating her pussy like he was on his way to the death chamber, and she was his last meal.

Trina, being the freak she was for her man, had raised up so she could watch Smurf eat her out. She had grabbed the back of his head and was grinding her pussy on his face while she encouraged him on.

"Damn, baby, you got me so wet. Right there, ooh shit, yes, I'm finna cum. I'm finna cum, baby. Suck on it hard. Just like that. Oh shit, I'm cumming!" she screamed before busting her nut all over his tongue and face.

"You woke the baby up," Smurf said, hearing his daughter crying in the other room.

"She just hungry. I'm finna go feed her in a minute. Come on, give me some of that dick real quick so I can go feed her," Trina said, climbing on top of him.

Chapter 22

Later that night, Smurf, Yakki, and Tiger were running around collecting money from all the spots they had fronted dope to.

"Let's go over to the spot I got my kinfolk in and count the bread. I need to drop them off this package anyway," Yakki said.

"Let's roll," Tiger said. "We closer to your spot than we is to the condo anyway."

Smurf headed that way, and in ten minutes, they were pulling up in front of Yakki's spot. Before they could get out the truck and into the spot, five cars had pulled up and been served.

"Damn, bro, this bitch rolling like a muthafucka," Smurf said.

"I told you, this is a million-dollar spot," Yakki agreed.

"What all they working with in there?" Smurf asked.

"Shit, they got everything. Crack, powder, pills, Dro, Kush, Ice, and I let them niggas have the dip. So, they making a killing off the dip, and they split the profit between them. They still getting their cut off everything else, but I let them niggas have the money off the dip. I gotta keep them niggas happy, ya dig?" Yakki told them.

"You ain't did nothing wrong right here. Tell them niggas to get some heroin and run that too. This a nice little block, and it's a quiet street. You can run this bitch for the next five years if them young niggas don't get goofy and start shooting niggas and make the block hot. You know how Baby Boy can get. That's a wild-ass young nigga," Tiger said.

"I already told that hot-headed ass nigga the same thing," Yakki assured him.

They got out the truck and went to the door. Knocky answered the door with a .40 Glock in his hand, with an extended clip and a lot of silver ornaments on it. The gun was a collector's edition that Knocky never left home without.

"What's up, cuz?" he said, stepping to the side and letting them in.

"Ain't shit, we just stopped by to drop y'all this package off and handle some business," Yakki said. He, Smurf, and Tiger were each carrying a duffle bag. Yakki gave one of the duffle bags to Buckwheat. Baby Boy and Lil J were playing the PlayStation.

"We finna go upstairs and handle this business. Where Brandi at?" Yakki asked.

"She out on the block handling her business," Baby Boy answered.

They went upstairs and started separating the money and counting it.

"Let's count this bag first. This the only one that all three of us gotta split. The other bag is me and Smurf's," Tiger said.

They counted the money, and it came out to be eight hundred thousand and six hundred dollars. They split that up into three equal amounts and started counting the other bag. It came out to one point three million. Smurf and Tiger split that up. While they were counting the money, Baby Boy came upstairs and brought them some smoke and a bottle of Patron.

"Cuz, I know y'all need this, the way y'all working up here," Baby Boy said, handing them the bottle and the bag of smoke.

"Appreciate that, cuz. Counting the money harder than making the money," Yakki said, and they all busted out laughing.

"Holla if y'all need something else," Baby Boy said, heading back downstairs.

"If you can keep that young nigga on his hustle and off that tough-guy shit, always shooting niggas and shit, you might got you something going," Tiger said.

"I know, I gotta keep the nigga mind on the bag and off the trigger," Yakki said.

They drove to the club and went in through the back door. It was a weeknight, but the club was still jumping. During the weekdays, they had karaoke night and half-price drinks. The club was somewhat packed, but it was an older crowd with mostly women.

They had a few drinks and smoked a couple of blunts in the private VIP area, while watching the crowd and enjoying the music.

"Cuz, it's almost 1:00 AM. I better get to the house before I have to kick Cassie's ass. She gon' swear I was out in the streets fucking around," Yakki said.

As soon as he finished talking, his phone started ringing. He looked at the screen and saw it was Cassie. "This her calling right now," he said, showing them the phone.

"What's up, baby?" he answered.

He listened for a few minutes before he said, "I'm at the club with Smurf and Tiger, we about to leave right now. I'll be home in a few." He listened for a few before he said, "Okay, I love you too. Alright, bye."

"Come on, let's go before we get this nigga in trouble," Smurf said, joking with his day one.

"Y'all niggas got me fucked up," Yakki said after Tiger and Smurf started laughing at him. "I run my house, Cassie know who run this shit," Yakki said, trying to act tough.

"Yeah, yeah, yeah, we know who run the shit too. CASSIE!"

"Tender dick-ass nigga," Tiger added.

Chapter 23

"Cuz, them niggas just counted about five million right here in our spot," Baby Boy told Buckwheat, Lil J, and Knocky.

"I been trying to tell y'all niggas that them niggas crumbing us," Buckwheat said. "We just split up three hundred thousand between us, and them niggas split up five million. How that add up, and we doing all the dirty work? If the laws run up in this bitch right now, ain't none of them niggas going to jail, we is, and them niggas gonna still be out here getting money and fucking bitches."

"Bro, we making a hundred stacks or more every three or four days. How them niggas crumbing us?" Lil J asked.

"Bro, that ain't shit, cuz, when them niggas making millions. They ain't doing shit. We sitting up in this bitch taking all the risk," Buckwheat continued.

"So what we 'pose to do about it?" Lil J asked. "We just gotta hustle harder."

"That nigga Buckwheat right for the first time in his life. Cuz crumbing us. Them niggas just counted five mill and we made a hundred stacks a piece. That's not even ten percent of what them niggas made. I'm really starting to get heated now that I think about it. Cuz really trying to play us like we some ho-ass niggas, bird feeding a nigga like that," Baby Boy said.

"Them niggas had to put in work to get to the point where they pulling in a mill. That nigga Yakki didn't jump off the porch getting paper like that. I remember five or six years ago when that nigga was driving that old-ass Lac. Smurf didn't even have a ride; he was using his brother's shit. We gon' get our paper up, we just gotta put in a little work, just like they did," Lil J tried reasoning with them. He already knew where the conversation was leading, dealing with his cousin Baby Boy.

"Man, cuck all that friendly shit, that nigga tried to play us like some suckas. I ain't nobody sucka! That nigga ain't getting a dime outta this drop. Matter of fact, he ain't getting another dime outta this spot. This my spot now!" Baby Boy told them, heated.

"I'm with you all the way on that, cuz. The nigga really handling us on some smooth, sneak shit. That's y'all kinfolk too, I can't believe he would do family like that," Buckwheat said, making Baby Boy even madder.

"What we suppose to tell the nigga when he come to get his money? Cuz ain't going for no bullshit about his bread," Lil J told them.

"Cuz, fuck that nigga! I'll murk that nigga. Is you down with us, or is you on that nigga side? He fucking over you too, nigga," Baby Boy said.

"It's whatever," Lil J gave in, not wanting to go against his crew even when he knew they were wrong.

"Now that's the J I know. What up with you, Knocky?" Baby Boy asked.

"I'm on go at all times. I don't give a fuck," Knocky said, clutching his beloved nine with the silver ornament on it.

"Cuz, since we going all in like that, we might as well hit them niggas hard. Let's follow this nigga Smurf and rob his bitch ass too. All them niggas fair game, Tiger too," Buckwheat said.

"Hell yeah, let's get his bitch ass too," Baby Boy agreed.

"Y'all niggas hold the spot down while me and Knocky follow this nigga Smurf. If Yakki come by while we gone, get the drop on the nigga and tie his bitch ass up until we get back," Baby Boy instructed.

A few nights later, Baby Boy and Knocky had been following Smurf all day. Smurf was in a black Suburban with tinted windows. He had been riding around all day with Tiger. They'd went shopping and drove out to Lake Dallas to check on some property Tiger wanted them to buy.

After checking on the property, they had gone to Fort Worth and picked up a hundred and eighty thousand from a nigga they had fronted some work to.

"Let's go to Spanky's and shoot some pool and have a few beers," Tiger said.

Smurf drove over to the bar, and they went inside and shot pool for a couple of hours.

"It's almost midnight. I gotta get to the house before Trina starts tripping. I told her I was gonna start trying to come in before twelve. I gotta start helping her with the baby."

"Shit, let's go, I'm ready to hit the shower and go to sleep," Tiger answered.

"I gotta drop you off, and I still gotta stop by the club and give that bread to Junior."

After dropping Tiger off, Smurf drove to the club. He parked at the back by the private entrance they used. He got out the truck and reached back in to get the money that was in a paper sack on the back seat. He felt the barrel of a gun in his side and heard a nigga say, "Let me get that bread up off you, homie," Knocky said as he put the gun against Smurf's back.

When he saw that Smurf was on his way to the club, he knew he was dropping off some money.

"Bro, you gon' have to slide up on the nigga. We got these disguises on, but that nigga gon' know it's me, cause I'm a lil nigga. Can you handle it?" Baby Boy asked.

"I got it, my nigga. I hope this nigga don't make me pop his ass. You already know I don't play or repeat myself. That's your cousin, you sure you want me to go?"

"Do whatever you gotta do to get back to this car uninjured," Baby Boy answered.

Smurf had just reached in the truck and got the bag of money when he felt the gun against his back and heard the voice behind him.

"You got it, my nigga," Smurf said as he dropped the bag on the ground, turning slightly around so he could see who was behind him.

He saw a nigga a little taller than him with a ski mask on. When the nigga bent to pick up the bag, Smurf kneed him in the face and grabbed the pistol. For a minute, they struggled over the gun before it went off, and Smurf heard the muffled blast of a shot and felt the bullet that struck him in the hand.

Smurf kept hold of the barrel of the gun until he finally snatched it out the nigga's hand, and it clattered to the ground.

Smurf pushed the nigga off of him and dove for the pistol. When he stood back up with the gun, the nigga was running away with the bag. Smurf tried to shoot the nigga in the back, but his hand wouldn't work, and he dropped the pistol. By the time he picked the gun back up, he heard tires burning rubber. He threw the pistol in his truck and looked at his hand. It was covered in blood, and he saw a small hook in the palm and a slightly larger hole in the back of his hand.

He found a clean towel in the back of the truck and wrapped it around his hand. He got in the truck and called Tiger and Yakki.

"Some niggas robbed me in the parking lot at the club," he told Tiger, who he called first.

"Where you at right now?" Tiger asked.

"In my truck, still in the parking lot. I'm finna drive to the emergency room."

"They jumped you or what?"

"Naw, they shot me in the hand."

"I'm on my way. What hospital you going to?" Tiger asked.

"Medical Center, the closest."

"On the Lane and 75?"

"Yeah."

"I'm on the way."

"Hey, call Trina and let her know I'm alright and to come too."

"I'm on it. I'll meet you there in a few."

"Right on."

He hung up with Tiger and called Yakki and told him the same thing before he drove to the emergency room.

By the time he got to the emergency room, his hand was hurting. He looked at it and thought he saw small pieces of bone sticking out of the exit wound hole. He tried making a fist but couldn't, and a sharp pain shot from his hand all the way up his shoulder. The pain was so intense that it made him dizzy. He had to sit back in the car seat for a minute until his head cleared before he could finally get out of the car and walk into the hospital.

Smurf opened his eyes in a hospital room with Trina sitting next to the bed, and Omar, Zell, and Tiger were all in the room.

"What happened?" he asked.

"You got robbed and shot. You don't remember anything?" Tiger answered and asked.

As soon as Tiger said it, the memories started coming back, and the whole incident started replaying in his mind. He shook his head, letting Tiger and Omar know that he would tell them about it when Trina and Zell left the room.

He looked at his heavily bandaged hand and asked Trina, "What did they do to my hand?"

"The bullet broke some bones, so they had to go in and clean it out and put some pins and screws in your hand. The doctor said you will be alright."

"How long I gotta stay here? I'm ready to get the fuck outta here. I hate hospitals."

"They were just waiting on you to wake up. Let me go get the nurse and tell her you are ready to go," Trina said, getting up and leaving the room.

Zell, being wise and on game, knew that they wanted to talk alone and said, "Well, I guess I will go out to the waiting room and see how everyone is doing and let them know you are alright. It's somebody we know cause the nigga parked on the side of the building that don't have a camera. It was two niggas, and only one got out. Junior said he saw a black Tahoe leaving, but you can't tell who the niggas are."

"Do we know anybody that got a black Tahoe?" Tiger asked.

"Let's get the fuck outta here and get everyone together, then we'll find out something," Omar said, calling Slime.

"Blood, I need everybody at the club, emergency meeting, in two hours. Every muthafucka that claim MOB or under this umbrella need to be there."

"I'm on it, OG."

Chapter 24

Yakki was out in the waiting room watching everyone to see if he saw anything suspicious. It was almost twenty people there in support of Smurf. Little did Yakki know, Em, J-Low, and K-Rock were doing the same thing.

"Come on, y'all, he's coming out now," Zell informed everyone.

Yakki saw a nurse pushing Smurf down the hallway in a wheelchair with Tiger and Omar following.

"What you doing in a wheelchair, cuz?" Yakki asked.

"That's the policy at the hospital — they gotta push a nigga out like this. Go get the truck," Smurf said, throwing Yakki the keys.

They got Smurf into the passenger seat of the truck. Yakki got behind the wheel, and Tiger got in the backseat after giving his keys to Em so she could drive his car. They were all headed to the club for the meeting.

"I can't believe them niggas would pull some shit like this in our city. Cuz, if it's the last thing I do, I'ma find the niggas responsible and murk every nigga involved," Yakki said, getting heated.

"We gon' murk every nigga involved," Tiger added.

"Cuz, whoever them niggas is, they weak as fuck. I took that nigga's gun, cuz. Fuck — them niggas thought they was fucking with me? Like I'ma lay down and give up my shit like a bitch? Nigga, I'm real stepper. I been steppin' on shit since I jumped off the porch," Smurf said while reaching under the passenger seat and getting the gun he took from the robber.

"I took that nigga's gun, cuz," he said, showing Tiger and Yakki the gun.

When Yakki looked over and saw the gun, he almost ran off the road.

"Cuz, where you get that gun?" Yakki asked in shock.

"Nigga, I just told you — I took this bitch from the nigga that shot me."

Tiger, hearing the surprise in Yakki's voice, asked, "You know that gun or something?"

"Cuz, that's that nigga Knocky's gun."

"You talkin' about that lil nigga that's over at your spot with your cuzzin'?" Smurf asked.

"Yeah, cuz," Yakki said, shaking his head, confused.

"Naw, my nigga — that nigga wouldn't disrespect like that," Smurf said, not wanting to believe they would test his gangsta.

"Cuz, that's that nigga heat. I done saw that nigga with that bitch too many times with all that silver shit on it. I just saw it the other night when we was over there counting that bread."

"You sure, my nigga?" Tiger asked.

Before Yakki could answer, his phone started ringing.

"Hello?"

"What up, Brandi?" Yakki said.

"Hey — don't go over to that spot. Them fools on some fuck shit. They talkin' about killin' you. Baby Boy started all this shit. I just heard them talkin' about killin' you and they not gonna pay you for the work they sellin'. They gon' kill you when you go back over there to get the money. So if they call you talkin' about bringin' some more work, don't go — they plottin'. I'm not goin' back over there."

"That's good lookin' out. I appreciate the heads up. I'ma come by your spot later on and fuck with you. A'ight, one," he said, disconnecting the call.

106

"It was them niggas," Yakki said to Smurf and Tiger. "Brandi just told me she overheard the niggas plottin' to down me when I go back over there."

"Cuz, was you breakin' bread with them niggas righteous shit?" Tiger asked.

"Cuz, them niggas got half of everything they sold out the spot and they were hustlin' they won shit too and I wasn't getting nothing off they shit. Them niggas greedy and snakes."

"I'ma murk every one of them lil niggas — one by one or all at the same time. I don't give a fuck. But them niggas not livin' in this city no more," Smurf said, watching Yakki's reaction outta the corner of his eye 'cause he knew that Baby Boy and Lil J was his relatives.

Before Yakki could respond, Tiger said, "Nigga, you been fuckin' up for the last year. You bringin' a lot of drama to the operation. Is you back smokin' that shit?"

"Don't disrespect me like that, OG," Yakki said, looking Tiger in his eyes through the rearview mirror. "I know you upset, but I ain't the enemy. I'm as fucked up as you are, and when we handle these niggas my gun gonna bust just as many times as yours is, relatives or not. I don't give a fuck. Them niggas disrespected and they gotta go. Cuz spoke on it and that law. They gotta go. And to answer your question — naw, my nigga, I ain't back on shit."

Tiger nodded, respecting how Yakki came, and said, "Let's handle these niggas then and get this shit over with so we can get back to the money."

"That's the same thing I was thinkin', OG."

Chapter 25

They made it to the club and went inside. Not too many people had shown up yet, but Slime and some of his people were sitting around, having drinks and smoking.

"We really don't need to have this meeting since we figured out who's responsible and we gonna handle them niggas ourselves," Tiger said.

"Yeah, you right. Let me go find Omar and let him know so he can call the meeting off," Smurf agreed.

Smurf went upstairs and found Omar in the office with Junior and Em, looking at the surveillance tapes. He explained everything to him, and Omar told Em to call the meeting off. Em immediately got on the phone and made a few calls.

"Look, you can't see shit on the other side of the club. That's a complete blind spot. I can't believe you haven't noticed that. Bro, you are the manager of the club, you gotta see shit like this before something happens. Get someone out here to put some cameras on that side of the club. Matter of fact, get all those cheap-ass cameras replaced with some high-definition cameras so we can see. You really can't see shit outta those cheap-ass cameras."

"Em, you over security, so it ain't all on Junior. You should have seen this too. Y'all got the budget and the authority to do anything you need to do to protect our establishment and our people. Those cameras should have been replaced. We can't call ourselves a high-quality club with shit like that. Em, check everything we own, get the cameras replaced everywhere if they need replacing, and make sure the whole property can be seen—no more blind spots," Omar said, still looking at the cameras.

Em had already gotten on the phone and given instructions to her team. She had hired three people, including K-Rock's friend Shelly, who worked at the agency with her and had set up the listening device for them in Florida.

Em had talked her into coming to Dallas and working with them. Shelly had just finished doing the property out at Omar's new place.

"Smurf, we all finna go out to check it. I need you to come too. You ain't had a chance to see what it look like now that all the construction workers are gone."

"Let's roll, we gonna follow you," Smurf said.

When they got out there, Smurf could see that the whole property was surrounded by black iron and white stone security gates. At the entrance were huge black gates that Omar opened with a remote. There was a gatehouse, but there was also a keypad that would open the gate when no one was in the gatehouse.

"Look at this shit, cuz. This is beautiful. This how a nigga's supposed to be living. And to think this nigga grew up in the hood on the block. I helped raise this young nigga," Tiger said proudly.

"Man, this some movie-type shit. Right on the lakefront," Smurf said.

"I gotta get Cassie a house like this," Yakki added.

"This what we do this shit for, so a nigga can live like this. Now, this some real live living, and the nigga made it out the game without the FEDS fucking with him," Tiger added.

The main house had six wings that led to six homes. Each home had either five or six bedrooms and was connected to the main house by a hallway or courtyard that each house opened onto.

There were six other guest houses that came with the property and four more that had been recently built, scattered around the ten acres.

After everyone had gotten out of the cars, Omar said, "We finna celebrate. Y'all get Trina and Cassie out here. In the meantime, y'all walk around and check out everything. If y'all want, you can take the boat out on the lake or fish off the dock. Whatever you wanna do, just enjoy yourselves." Once Omar was done talking, he disappeared into the house.

Tiger and Smurf spent the day playing and talking to Shayla. They took her out on the boat and showed her how to fish. She caught her first fish, which scared the hell out of her when the fish bit her hook. Smurf had to reel the fish in for her.

"Hey, you caught your first fish!" Tiger told her proudly.

"What you wanna do with it, Shayla? You wanna cook it and eat it?" Smurf asked.

"No," she said, shaking her head, trying to get away from the squirming fish.

"Well, what you wanna do with it?" Smurf asked.

"Throw it back in the water," she said.

"You sure you don't want Zell to cook it for you?"

"No, throw it," she said, pointing to the water.

Shayla kept on fishing and caught three more fish. She threw every one of them back in the lake. She was laughing and having fun with her dad and big brother. They spent the whole day with her, something they hadn't done in a long time.

Chapter 26

Later, the barbecue grills were going, and the guests started arriving. Tables had been set up in the courtyard, and Glenn, Jay, and Pops were grilling the meat.

Omar sat with his mom, Connie, Zell, Shalika, and Yolonda. They were having drinks and enjoying small talk. Some people were eating while others were smoking and having drinks.

Omar had invited all of his best friends. Zell had even invited her mom and stepdad. Since the wedding, they had kind of reconciled and were back on speaking terms. Omar had encouraged Zell to make things right with her mom.

After everyone had eaten and were in a mellow mood, Zell got up and spoke. "Excuse me, excuse me, can I have a few minutes of your time? I promise I won't take all night. I want to thank all of you for coming to our housewarming get-together. We wanted to make this a special night and spend it with our friends and family. So again, thank you guys for coming, and now I would like to call my wonderful husband up here to say a few words to you all. Thank you."

"Okay," Omar started. "Thank all of y'all for coming. When we bought this place, I just wanted somewhere outta the city for us to live quietly. Then one night while me and Zell were here alone, I started thinking about everything that had taken place in the last year with Dre and Rob, other people we lost, and the new lives that we brought in and that are on the way. I started thinking, life is short. We spend all our lives chasing the money, then when you get it, you don't know what to do with it. I lost three of my best friends—Lil Chris, Big Dre, and Rob." His voice started cracking, and Zell, Shalika, and Yolonda went and stood by him. Zell whispered something in his ear, and he nodded and continued. "I just knew that I wanted to be able to spend as much time as I could around the people that I loved. So that's why we added ten houses to the property."

"Now, before I go any further, I have some special guests I want to call out. Y'all come on out," Omar said, and out of the doors of the main house walked Chief and Pecas.

"Oh shit, not my niggas!" Smurf said, jumping up and running over to embrace them. Lisa, Dub, Bobi, D-Money, and Yakki were right behind him.

"Now, y'all bear with me a few more minutes. Mama and Pops, this is for y'all," Omar said, and Zell handed them a set of keys with a door number on it. "This is your house from me and my family."

"Thank you, baby," Faye said, hugging him. Pops came up, shook his hand, and hugged him for a long moment, thanking him also.

"Naw, thank you, Pops, for being a father to another nigga's kids, and Mama, you the best mother a nigga could ever want, need, or have. Y'all right next door, so keep the noise down when you and Pops be doing what y'all be doing at night," Omar said, laughing.

"Boy, shut your nasty ass up," Faye said, blushing.

"All right, all right, Connie, this is for you, big sis. I love you, girl, and I don't get to see enough of you. Now, I'll be able to see you every day." Shalika handed her a set of keys.

"Thank you, and I love you too," she said, kissing Omar on the cheek.

"Junior, Dell, and Jay, these y'all's," Omar paused while Zell, Shalika, and Yolonda took them the keys. "I love y'all, bro."

"We love you too," they said in unison.

"Glenn just got a house built in Rockwall on Lake Ray Hubbard, so he didn't want to give that up and come out here with us," Omar said, sounding sad.

"Lil bro, I'ma be out here so much, you gon' get tired of me. I have four brothers and a sister with houses out here, I can sleep in a different house every night, and you know I'ma stay sleeping at Jay's house," Glenn said.

"Damn!" Jay said, making everybody laugh.

"Dub, D-Money, and Bobi, these y'all's," Omar said as the ladies took them the keys. "Man, Lil Chris—"

"Come on, big bro, don't start with that. We know," Dub said, interrupting him before he made everybody sad.

"All right."

"Thank you, my nigga," Bobi said, and they all came and gave Omar a hug.

"Em, K-Rock, J-Low, these keys to the main house. Y'all have a whole wing to yourselves. Y'all not going nowhere. Come on up here." Omar, Zell, Shalika, and Yolonda hugged each one of them as he handed them each a set of keys.

"Smurf and Trina, y'all come on up here and get these keys," Omar said, giving them each a set of keys.

"Thank you, Omar," Trina said, giving him all a hug.

"Deuce, deuce to the roof!" Smurf said, throwing up the hood and giving Omar a hug.

Shayla came running up, naked. "You gonna be living with us?"

"Yep, me and Trina."

"Come on, let's go look at your house," she said, trying to pull Smurf away.

"Hold on, hold on, we gonna go check it out in a minute."

"Yakki and Cassie, y'all come on up here and get these keys. You too, OG Tiger, we bringing the hood to the lakefront," Omar said, throwing up the hood.

"We got the whole hood out here. Thank you, bro," Yakki said.

Cassie gave Omar a hug and said something in Spanish as he gave her the keys.

"Translation?" Omar said, smiling.

"She said a prayer for all of us," Yakki informed him.

"Oh, okay."

"Brazy, come on up here and bring them kids with you," Omar said, giving him a set of keys.

"Thanks, OG," Brazy said, locking up with him.

"Thank you, Uncle Omar," Kay said.

"Thanks, Unk. What school we gon' be going to? I hope they got a basketball team," Trey said.

"Your game ain't bad like that," Omar said, joking with Trey. He already knew Trey was ranked as one of the top young players in the country. He was just thirteen and already six feet tall.

"I'm going to the NBA, Uncle Omar, watch."

"Well, if you don't like the school out here, we gonna find you a prep school or something. Holla at your daddy and get it understood, and I got you," Omar assured him.

"Thanks, Unk."

"Tyrone, these kids so nice. Yo' bad ass wasn't nothing like this when you were little," Faye said.

Brazy couldn't do nothing but shake his head and smile.

"George and Kawanna, y'all come on up here. That's all right, Kawanna, you stay seated. You look like you 'bout to have that baby at any minute. George, bring yo' ugly ass on up here."

"My baby ain't ugly," Kawanna yelled.

"Okay, sister-in-law," he said to her and gave George the keys. "I love you, bro, and I put yo' ass right next to Brazy so he can bug you every day like he did when we was locked up," Omar said, laughing.

"Thanks, bro," George said and pointed at the sky. Then he whispered, "Big Dre, fat ass, watching us."

"Fa sho," Omar said, giving him a hug. George still hadn't gotten over Dre's death.

"Last but not least, to two of the realest niggas that ever walked the streets of Dallas, Texas. Chief and Pecas, come on up here and get these keys."

Chief was so drunk his wife, Kim, had to come up and get the keys while cussing him out in Spanish.

"Thank you, big brother," she said, taking the keys and giving him a hug.

Pecas was drunk too. But he could drink all day and never be sloppy drunk. Omar gave him the keys, and 'P' grabbed him in a bear hug.

"Thanks, bro, from me and my family," he said, pointing to his wife and their two kids. "I got one thing to say, Glenn and Jay, there's some Mexicans part of the family now. Y'all gotta learn how to cook some muthafuckin' tacos," he said and let out one of those crazy-ass Mexican yells.

"We got you, bro," Glenn said, laughing.

"Okay, we almost done. I just have a few more things to say and we can get back to the festivities. No drugs come on this property other than your recreational personal weed or whatever. Also, I know some of y'all may want your parents out here with you or other family members. I own thirty acres. If you want to have them a house built at your own expense, come holla at me and we can make it happen. That's it, let's enjoy the rest of the night," Omar said.

Chapter 27

While everyone was enjoying the night, Omar and Zell walked around looking over the property and discussing how the night went.

"Baby, I have all the people around me that I love, but you don't have any of your friends out here with you," he said.

"I don't really have any friends."

"What about your mom and your sister?"

"Hell to the no on my mom. She would bring her husband with her, and he's a racist prick. She has the same views as he does. I don't want that kind of negativity around me, my family, or our friends. I'm happy talking to her on the phone on Christmas and birthdays."

"My sister . . . we have never been close. I haven't talked to her in years. The last I heard from her, she was still in the Middle East somewhere on a ship in the middle of the sea. She's never going to leave the navy."

"Well, what about Kyra, her husband, and their kids? And Darla is your best friend?"

"I could ask them and see if they wanted to come out here."

"The night is still young; it's barely 7:00 p.m. Call them and get them out here."

"Well, let me see," she said, pulling out her phone and making the calls. After a few minutes on the phone, she hung up and said, "Well, that was easy. I had to trick them. I told them I needed them to get out here as fast as they could. It's very important. They were worried, but I assured them I was all right. I just needed them to come out here. They should be here within the next hour."

"Okay, let's walk down by the lake," Omar said, grabbing her hand. "Hey, I need you to be more vocal with your needs and wants. I can't think of everything, and sometimes small things may slip my mind or I may completely overlook things, not intentionally. But I need you to help me."

"I had been meaning to ask you about your friends and if you wanted to invite anyone out here. But things got to moving so fast with what happened to Smurf, I completely forgot. I apologize for that."

"All of this," he said, waving his hand around, "half of it is yours. Talk to me and let me know what you are feeling and what you want to do. I cherish your input. Okay?" He lifted her head and kissed her, while at the same time pulling her to him and squeezing her ass.

"Oh God, I love it when you do that."

"What?"

"Everything. Talk like that, kiss me like that, and I really love it when you squeeze my ass like that. Do it again."

"Like this?" he said, pulling her to him, squeezing her ass, and lifting her up. She put her arms around his neck and wrapped her legs around his waist while he held her up by her ass. He looked into her eyes for a long moment before he finally kissed her passionately.

"I want to marry you," she said when he put her back on the ground.

"We're already married," he said, laughing.

"I know. But I love you so much I want to marry you again, and again, and again. I want to renew our vows every year until the day I die."

"Okay, if that's what you want to do, I'm with it," he said, kissing her again.

"That's what I want to do," she answered. "Now come over here behind those trees, I wanna suck your cock," she said, grabbing his hand and pulling him behind a patch of trees.

"Damn, I love this white woman," he thought as she led him behind the trees.

When they finally made it back inside, Slime, Lisa, and Darla were already there. Darla was a thick blonde, divorced, with two kids, a girl and a boy around Danielle's age. Darla was a school teacher who had worked with Zell.

"Hey, Darla," Omar spoke, giving her a hug before leaving her and Zell alone so they could talk.

He walked over to where Lisa and Slime stood talking.

"What's up, y'all?" he said, hugging Lisa and locking up with Slime.

"I had to follow Slime out here. You know I ain't good with directions. You have it looking good out here," Lisa said.

"Thanks. That's what I wanted to talk to you and Slime about," he said, reaching in his pocket and pulling out two sets of keys. "This for you." He handed one set of keys to Slime. "The door number is on the key. That's your house, Blood. Everybody moving out here."

"OG, thanks. I appreciate this. Let me go check out the pad, and I got someone I want you to meet when I come back."

"All right. Here, Lisa," he said, offering a set of keys to her.

"Hey, Big Bro," Brazy said, stopping him from giving the keys to Lisa. "That's what I wanted to talk to you about."

"What's up, Dawg?"

"Uhh, Lisa was going to move in with me and the kids if that's all right with you," Brazy said.

"Hell yeah, it's all right with me if that's what y'all want," he said, looking at Lisa.

"That's fine with me. Let me ask y'all a question. Are y'all together in a relationship?"

"Bro, I think we about to get married. The kids love her and Kay's crazy about the baby."

"Y'all serious, huh?"

They both said "Yeah" at the same time and started blushing.

Omar knew then that they were serious. "Well, y'all have my blessing. When y'all plan on getting married?"

"We hadn't set a date yet. Lisa's been so busy with the record label and trying to get Yolonda's album finished. Then she just signed this new lil nigga named Franki. We gonna get it done as soon as we get some time."

"Me and Zell gonna renew our vows here at the house. Y'all can do it then if you want to. Lisa, you can get with Zell and coordinate the colors or whatever. You know, the girl stuff, and me and my nigga, we gonna pay for it," Omar said, giving Brazy a handshake.

"I'll get with Zell, that would be perfect," Lisa said.

Omar saw that Kyra had arrived and was talking to Zell and Darla. He said, "I'm really happy for y'all. Let me go holla at Zell, I see she keep looking over here at me. Y'all fix yourselves something to eat and relax."

"He's on a diet," Lisa said.

"Fat-ass nigga," Omar said, shaking his head and laughing as he walked off. He couldn't wait to go tell George.

He went over and hugged and spoke to Kyra. "Hey, Kyra, where your ole man and the kids at?"

"They headed straight for the food."

"Let me go find them. You all right, baby?" he asked Zell. "You want something to drink or eat?"

"I'm fine, thank you."

"Call me if you need me," he said, kissing her before he walked off.

He was on his way to talk to George when he ran into Slime coming back from checking out the house. He was with a beautiful young lady that looked like she was Asian or at least mixed with Asian.

"OG, I wanted you to meet my friend, Im. Im, this is one of my best friends, Omar."

"I know who you are," she said, shaking his hand.

"You know me?" he asked, trying to place her.

"Yeah, I grew up on the Lane. I moved after my dad was killed back in the day. My dad was cool with you."

"Your dad? What was his name?"

"They called my dad Gat."

"Oh shit, I remember you. Some out-of-town niggas ran up in my nigga Gat's spot and robbed and killed him. Your mom and her people used to own the clothes and jewelry store right next to the cigarette plus on the corner of Audelia and the Lane."

Her dad Gat was an older cat, maybe a little younger than Omar's mom and Pops. He was a jack boy that robbed drug dealers in other cities and states. He would come back to Dallas and sell the drugs that he'd robbed niggas for to Omar.

Rumor had it that he had robbed some big-time dealers out of Houston, and they had tracked him down, ran up in his shit, and shot him up. He had killed a couple of them niggas too in the shootout before they had finally got him.

If he remembered correctly, she was supposed to have been hiding in the closet and witnessed the whole shootout. But Gat made her take his car and leave with the money before the cops came and he died.

"Yeah, that was my grandfather's store."

"Damn, what you been up to?"

"I moved out to the suburbs with my cousin and finished school. Now I'm at SMU studying criminal law."

"That's good. I used to fuck with OG Gat the long way. That was my nigga. If you need anything, all you gotta do is holla. Here, give me your phone so I can put my number in there." He dialed his number from her phone and saved his number in her phone, then saved hers in his. "What's your name again?"

"Im Yo Chick."

"I remember that last name Chick from the newspaper articles. Gat's real name was Alonzo Chick, or something like that. Right?"

"Yeah, that's it, Alonzo Chick."

"How is your mom doing?"

"She's all right. I just got back in contact with her about three years ago."

"That's good. That's good." He turned and said to Slime, "She's official, Dawg. Her pops was a real live 'G', original Lane nigga."

"Yeah, that's what she's been telling me."

Omar remembered that her grandfather had kidnapped her mom, his daughter, and sent her back to the Philippines or wherever they were from to get her away from Gat.

"It was nice seeing you again. Let me make a few rounds, and later on I have to introduce you to my wife. Where you staying? If you want to come out here with us, let me know. This family. Everybody from the Lane or lived on the Lane."

"I will call you and let you know something later on this week," she said as Omar was walking off.

Chapter 28

Omar went in search of George and found him sitting with Kawanna. She had her feet in his lap while he was massaging them.

"Bro, you'll never believe this," Omar started.

"What?"

"Brazy finna get married."

"To who?"

"Lisa," Kawanna spoke before Omar could answer.

"How you know?" they both asked, looking at her.

"All you have to do is pay attention. Look how they keep looking at each other and how close they stand to each other," she said.

Omar and George looked over at them for a few minutes and realized that, *if you watched them, you could tell.*

"Damn, I never even noticed it. But you can tell, huh?" Omar asked George.

"Yeah, you can. That fat-ass nigga in love," George said, laughing. "I'm happy for the nigga. Them kids need a mama. I know they tired of eating McDonald's and Churches every night," he added, and they both started laughing.

Zell walked up and sat down with them. "Are Tyrone and Lisa a couple?" she asked.

Omar and George looked at each other and bust out laughing.

"What's wrong?" Zell said, confused.

"Baby, we were just talking about that when you walked up. Kawanna spotted it too. But Brazy just told me. I offered her a set of keys, and they told me that she was moving in with Brazy and the kids."

"I'm happy for them," Zell said.

"I told Lisa that we were going to renew our vows, and she said that she was going to talk to you about that. I think they might want to get married at the same time."

"Ooh, that's a good idea. Y'all have room for us? We wanna renew our vows too," Kawanna asked.

"I was thinking about doing it right here in this courtyard, if that's all right with you, baby?" Omar asked Zell.

"I was thinking the same thing. Of course, we have room for y'all. I think a lot of people are going to join in once they find out what we are going to do."

"Come on, let's go find Danielle. I need to talk to her," Omar said, taking Zell's hand. "I'll holla back at you later, bro," he told George as they walked off.

"Let me call her and see where she's at," Zell said.

"Tell her to meet us down by the lake."

"She on her way," Zell told him before she ended the call. "What's going on, baby?" Zell asked him before Danielle got there.

"Nothing for you to worry about. I just wanted to talk to her."

"Oh, I thought she did something," Zell finished saying just as Danielle walked up.

"Is everything alright? Did somebody else get shot?" Danielle asked with a worried look on her face.

"No, calm down. I just wanted to talk to you."

"Oh, okay. I'm here," she said impatiently.

"These are yours," Omar said, showing her a set of keys. "These are to the house next door to us. If you noticed, I didn't give that house to anyone." She nodded, and he continued, "I'm not going to give you the keys until after you and Dub decide what y'all gonna do. This has nothing to do with you and everything to do with him. I'm not going to make it easy for him. He has to make some type of commitment before y'all start living together in my house. Do you understand what I'm saying? I'm protecting you."

"I understand. You taught me better than that. I wasn't planning on living with him in any type of way until I got a lavish proposal and a ring," she said, smiling.

"That's how I like to hear you talk. If you want the keys now, you can have them, and you can move in right now if you want to get away from us that bad. But, I don't want him spending one night in that house until I'm satisfied that a wedding is coming," he told her.

"I'm fine where I'm at right now. I love being around my sisters and brothers. Shayla and Lil Omar would throw a fit if I tried to move out anyway. Not to mention King and Queen," she said, pointing.

Zell and Omar looked to where she pointed and saw the dogs hiding in the shadows, watching them. After they saw they had been spotted, they started sniffing the ground like they were looking for a place to use the restroom. They shook their heads and laughed.

"Smart-ass dogs," Omar said. "I just wanted to let you know that. Now, I need to go holler at Em and K-Rock. Have you seen Shalika and Yolonda?" he asked Danielle.

"They are both drunk. They were upstairs with me; we were about to watch a movie," she answered.

He leaned toward her and sniffed while she was talking and said, "Get your drunk butt on back up there with them."

"Unh-uhn, I'm not drunk."

"Unh-uhn, you are too," he said, laughing.

"Danielle," Zell said. "Well, baby, I guess I'm going upstairs to get drunk with the girls. I'll see you later."

"Okay, baby, I'll see you in a few," he said, kissing her and slapping her on the ass.

"Ewww, y'all nasty!" Danielle said.

Chapter 29

"Cuz, y'all some dumb-ass niggas! Both of y'all. Especially you, Baby Boy. You always wanna run some shit and don't know how to run nothing! You keep a nigga in some frivolous-ass bullshit," Lil J said heatedly after Knocky and Baby Boy came back and told them what happened.

"We was getting money! The most money a nigga had ever seen in our lives, and you dumb-ass niggas wanted to be greedy. Now, look what the fuck we done got ourselves into. Now, look what you nigga done got me into," Lil J continued, pacing the living room floor as he talked.

"How the fuck you let a nigga take your gun from you when you got the drop on that nigga and he ain't got no gun?" He paused. "Them niggas know that was your gun 'cause you always playing with that muthafucka like you just about that action."

"You ain't gon' pop nothing. You really a lil' scary-ass nigga riding Baby Boy's coattail, and he let you hang around 'cause he fucking yo' mama and both of your sisters."

"Cuz, don't be telling that nigga no shit like that," Baby Boy said.

"Shut the fuck up, nigga! I'm talking right now. When you was talking, you talked a nigga into this fuck shit. Now we all dead. Them niggas gon' kill all of us, and they know who we are, 'cause this lil' pussy-ass nigga let Smurf take his pistol," Lil J ranted.

"Say, cuz, I ain't gon' be too many more pussy-ass niggas," Knocky said, standing up.

"What you gon' do?" Lil J said as he continued to pace. When he got in reaching distance of Knocky, he threw a six-piece combination at him, dropping him to the floor. Then he started stomping and kicking him before Buckwheat and Baby Boy ran over and pulled him off Knocky.

"Come on, cuz, let's not start fighting each other," Buckwheat tried to reason with Lil J.

"Cuz, shut your bitch-ass up too," Lil J said, throwing a haymaker at Buckwheat that connected with his chin and knocked him out.

"Cuz, you trippin'," Baby Boy said.

"Naw, nigga, y'all tripped. Y'all wanna see me trip?" he asked, pulling out his gun and shooting Knocky five times in the face. *BOOM! BOOM! BOOM! BOOM! BOOM!* "Now I'm trippin'."

Baby Boy started slowly easing his hand towards his waistline where his strap was at.

"Go ahead, move your hand one more inch, nigga, and I promise you, kinfolk or not, I'ma blow your whole room off," Lil J assured him.

"Cuz, you trippin'."

"Nigga, stop talking to me," Lil J said. He went over to the table where they had been counting the money they had robbed for. It was a little over a hundred and eighty thousand. He grabbed fifty stacks and threw it at Baby Boy as hard as he could, then started putting the rest in his pockets.

"That bitch-ass nigga ain't gon' need his share," he said, pointing at Knocky. "And I'm taking that ho-ass nigga's share. I'm outta here," he added, walking out the front door and leaving it wide open.

Baby Boy got up and closed the door, locking it. He had already peeped Buckwheat watching J from the floor where he was laying before he walked out the door. Now, he was still laying in the same spot, faking. "Man, get your bitch-ass up and stop all that stuntin', scary-ass nigga, and help me get this nigga outta here."

"What we gon' do with this nigga, cuz?" he asked.

"We gon' wrap the nigga up in some sheets and shit, then carry the nigga out to yo' trunk and gon' dump the nigga's body somewhere in Oak Cliff or the South, somewhere, while I clean the spot up. Shit, we can't come back over here," he said, picking up the money off the floor and putting it in his pocket.

"Take this nigga to the after-hours spot on T.I. Blvd and dump him on the side of one of those buildings, and they'll think he got shot coming out the club or something. Shit, somebody get shot up there every other night. Take the sheets and shit off the nigga before you leave him." He thought about it for a minute and said, "Naw, I better go with your dumb ass to dump this nigga. Knowing you, you gon' do some dumb shit and have the laws looking for a nigga."

They wrapped the body in sheets and carried it out to Buckwheat's car. Baby Boy went back and locked the door. Then they drove over to the after-hours spot that was located in an isolated area with a lot of warehouses.

They carried the body behind one of the warehouses, took the sheets off, and laid him on the ground like he was running and had collapsed.

"That's about as good as it's gon' get," Baby Boy said. "Let's get the fuck outta here."

***

Brandi had been hiding in the closet at the spot for hours, listening to everything that was going on. She even heard when Lil J shot and killed Knocky.

When she'd left earlier, she had forgotten that her whole stash of dope and money were hidden in her room. She needed that. So she had come back and climbed through the window in her room and got stuck inside.

The condo had an alarm that beeped every time a door or window was opened. The patio door was open when she came back, so she was able to open her window and go inside. But when they started arguing, someone closed the patio door so the beeping stopped, and she was stuck.

If she opened the window, the beeping would start back, and they would know someone else was in the house with them. They were already on edge, and she had heard too much. She knew they would kill her.

So she did the only thing she could do: hide in the closet and pray that nobody came in and looked.

When she heard the room door open and saw through the closet door, Buckwheat came into her room, she pissed all over herself.

But when all he grabbed was the sheets and blankets off the bed, she was relieved and embarrassed. She sat in the closet with her head on her knees and her arms wrapped around her legs, crying and vowing that if the good Lord let her make it out alive, she was through running the streets and doing drugs.

The drugs that she had come back to get were in a plastic bag that she had put in her bra under her breasts. She took the bag out and emptied it out on the carpet floor in the closet and stepped on it, smashing it into the carpet.

When she heard them leave, she stayed in the closet, too scared to come out. Finally, she came out and went to the bedroom door, listening to make sure the place was empty. When she was convinced they were gone, she climbed back out the window, too scared to use the front door.

She ran to her car and got in. For a long time, she sat with her head on the steering wheel and cried before she pulled out her phone and called Yakki.

"They just killed Knocky," she cried into the phone when he answered.

"What are you talking about, Brandi?"

"They just killed Knocky at the spot."

"How you know that? I thought you left?"

"I did. I left my work and I came back to get it and got stuck in there. I had to hide in the closet until they left. I heard everything. They killed him," she said, starting to cry again.

"Calm down, calm down. Where you at right now?"

"I'm still right here in the parking lot in my car."

"Brandi, get the fuck out from over there."

Cassie was sitting next to him when he answered the phone. "Who the fuck are you talking to?" she asked, reaching for the phone.

"Calm down, Cassie."

"You talking to one of your bitches right in front of me, you disrespectful bastard," she said, getting loud.

Smurf, Tiger, and Omar were standing not too far away, and he waved them over, trying to ignore Cassie. Cassie started getting madder and louder 'cause he was ignoring her.

"Cassie, I'm finna slap the cowboy shit outta you if you don't sit down and shut the fuck up," he told her.

"What's up, cuz?" Smurf asked.

"Man, them niggas just killed Knocky at the spot. Brandi was hiding in the closet and heard the whole thing," he said, staring at Cassie with fire burning in his eyes.

"I thought she left?" Smurf asked.

"She did. She went back to get her dope and damn near got caught. She had to hide in the closet."

"Tell her to get the fuck from over there," Smurf said.

"Brandi—" he started to say, when she started to scream in his ear.

"Oh my God, noooooooo!"

"Brandi, what's wrong?"

"Yakki, two women just got in my car, and they got guns."

Em and K-Rock had been sitting outside in their car, watching the door. They had missed Baby Boy and

Buckwheat leaving, but they saw Brandi when she climbed out the window.

"Shhhh," Em said, putting two fingers up to her lips, getting in the passenger seat, and closing the door while K-Rock got in the back seat behind Brandi.

Em heard her call Yakki's name and reached over and took the phone from her. "Yakki, who is this white girl?"

"Who the fuck is this?"

"This is Em, Yakki."

"Em?"

"That's Em and K-Rock. I sent them over there to handle that situation," Omar told him.

"We need to get you away from here," Brandi told her.

She shook her head, no. "I need to go to rehab."

"I heard her," Yakki said, hearing her in the background. "Tell her I will come get her and take her to the same one I went to and where my mom is at."

She shook her head no after Em told her what he said. "If I don't go right now, I'm going to change my mind. I need to go right now."

"Take her," K-Rock said. "I'll stay here and watch the place. Call me when you get her situated."

"I appreciate y'all doing this for me. I'm about to call my caseworker and get everything set up. Take her to the same place I was at. It's right off Lemon and Turtle Creek."

Yakki made the call and got everything set up with his caseworker. The whole time, he was staring holes in Cassie. When he was done talking to the caseworker, he called Em back on Brandi's phone and told her that Lois Davenport would meet them at the rehab.

He told Brandi that he would bring her new clothes and everything else she needed the next day. "Just go in and get yourself together."

When he finally ended the call, he looked over at Cassie and said, "I need those keys that Omar gave you tonight and that ring on your finger."

"I'm sorry, Papi."

"The keys and the ring, Cassie."

When she still hesitated, he got up, went outside, got in his car and left.

Chapter 30

Baby Boy and Buckwheat were ducked off at the Budget Suites in Addison. Em and K-Rock had gotten a room at the same hotel and had been flirting with Buckwheat for the last three days.

They had finally talked him up to their room, making him think he was about to have a threesome. Em put a couple of drops of date rape drug in his drink, and when he woke up, he was hogtied at the same farm in Desoto that Short Dog had chopped Lil Murda's head off at.

"You are a dumb son of a bitch. Did you actually think that a lame-ass nigga like you would get some of this pussy?" Em said, laughing.

"Smurf is our little brother, asshole," K-Rock told him.

"I had nothing to do with that. You looking for Baby Boy and Knocky. They planned the whole thing. Knocky dead. Lil J already killed him. But Baby Boy was the nigga in the room with me," Buckwheat said, selling his homeboys out.

"We already know that," K-Rock told him, handing Em a long, wicked-looking knife like the one she already had in her hand.

"Tell us something we don't know," she said before she chopped his right arm off.

"Awwwwww," he screamed.

"You way out here in the country, can't nobody hear you," Em said, chopping his right arm off.

Blood squirting from where his arm used to be, he was screaming and hollering at the top of his voice.

"Please don't hurt me. I ain't had shit to do with nothing."

"Too late for that, buddy," Em said, chopping off one of his legs. K-Rock followed her lead and chopped off the other leg.

Buckwheat was screaming, begging, and pleading for them to kill him. K-Rock was laughing while she took the leg she had just cut off and whacked him upside the head with it.

"Shut the fuck up with all that, gangsta," she told him.

They used his phone and took several pictures of him with his arms and legs missing and sent them to Baby Boy and Lil J in a text message. Em also sent a recording of Buckwheat telling them that Baby Boy had set the whole play up.

When he had bled out and took his last breath, Em said, "Let's clean this shit up, feed this nigga to the pigs, and get the fuck outta here."

"I got one last surprise for these dumb-ass niggas," K-Rock told her, taking the knife she had and chopping his head off.

"I'ma take his head and leave it at the corner store where Smurf said them niggas used to hustle at," she said, giggling.

"Uh-uhn, bitch, you crazy as fuck," Em said.

"You gotta send a message to these wanna-be-ass niggas. Y'all not really gangsta, but we are."

That's the exact message she sent to Baby Boy and Lil J when she took pictures of Buckwheat's head sitting on the newspaper stand at the corner store in their hood in South Dallas.

Baby Boy and Lil J's phones were blowing up with people from the hood calling them to let them know that somebody had killed Buckwheat and left his head at the corner store.

One of the niggas had sense enough to get the head and throw it in the dumpster before somebody saw and called the laws.

Then the whole hood would be shut down, and there wouldn't be no hustling going on if one of those fools called the laws. It would be crime scene tape and homicide detectives all over, questioning niggas, and they didn't know shit.

Baby Boy called Lil J for the hundredth time and finally got an answer.

"What's up, cuz?" Baby Boy said.

"Fuck all that dumb shit. You see what you done got a nigga into with all that greedy-ass bullshit? Them niggas ain't playing no games, nigga. You see what they did to that nigga Buckwheat? I know they sent you the pictures too. That nigga was still alive with no legs or arms," Lil J said.

"Man, we was hiding out at the Budget Suites in Addison. That nigga met two bitches and went to their room and never came back, and the hoes missing too."

"I'm glad that nigga didn't know where I was. That ho-ass nigga went to telling everything he knew as soon as they got his scary ass."

"Cuz, I gotta get the fuck outta here. Where you at?" Baby Boy asked.

"Nigga, you gotta get that nigga Yakki that money back."

"I better not go nowhere close to them crazy-ass niggas."

"Cuz, take the money to your mama and call the nigga and let him know where the money at. Tell him that the nigga Knocky did that shit, and I smoked the nigga once we found out. I'll give you half the money back. Just do that and come to Shreveport."

"I'ma take care of it. I'll call you when I'm on my way."

"Cuz, don't let that nigga take you into meeting him anywhere. Put that money together, get it to your mom, make the call, and get the fuck out the city. Simple as that, and make sure they don't follow you down here."

"I got it, cuz."

Baby Boy ended the call and went to get the money together.

Chapter 31

Yakki had been laying low at his mom's house in his room. His mom was still at the rehab, so he had the house to himself. It had been two weeks since he had talked to anyone. His phone was off, lying somewhere on the floor. He'd been drunk for the whole two weeks.

He couldn't get Cassie out of his mind. She had acted a fool and embarrassed him in front of all of his friends. He was mad as fuck at her. So mad that he had told her to give him his ring back.

But he couldn't deny the fact that he loved her crazy ass, and he missed her. He couldn't close his eyes without her smell, her taste, and her touch invading his senses.

He thought he was hearing voices when he kept hearing someone call his name.

"This shit bad," he said, talking out loud to the bottle of vodka he was drinking from. "Got a nigga hearing voices."

He saw something move out of the corner of his eye and realized that he wasn't alone—someone else was in the house. He started reaching for his gun that was on the nightstand next to his bed, but he was so drunk that he fell off the bed, dropping the bottle of vodka.

He tried to get up but couldn't make it. He just laid there, waiting on whoever was in the house to go ahead and finish him off.

He thought he heard a female voice mumbling in Spanish. Then, he saw Mama Marcy, Cassie's mom, come around the side of the bed, shaking her head.

"Hey, Mama Marcy," he slurred, looking up from the floor.

She whispered something in Spanish to herself before leaning over and helping him back onto the bed. He fell several times before she was able to get him on the bed. She picked the half-filled bottle of vodka up and set it on the table next to the bed.

"This is nonsense. What are you doing to yourself?" she asked, waving her hand around the room at the bottle of alcohol and at him.

"Ca-, Ca-, Cassie—" he slurred, and started bawling like a baby. Marcy sat down on the side of the bed, and Yakki laid his head in her lap. She tried comforting him as he cried. The whole time, he was naked as the day he was born.

"Cassie is at the new house waiting on you to come home," Marcy told him.

"She hurt me, Ma. She don't trust me. She made me look like a fool in front of all my friends. That's—that's embarrassing."

"That's part of being in love. You haven't been on your best behavior the last year. But, she never left you; she stayed by your side. She nursed you and protected you until you were able to protect yourself."

She realized after a while that she was talking to herself when she heard Yakki snoring and felt his warm breath between her legs. She felt herself starting to get aroused and tried to move. But every time she attempted to move, Yakki would grab her and start mumbling in his sleep.

She sat back and gave in to the sensation that his warm breath was sending through her body. His snoring sent vibrations straight to her pussy. After several minutes, she had an orgasm so intense that her body started shaking, and her juices flowed so much that her pants were soaked.

Yakki, with his face between her legs even in his slumber, smelled the aroma of fresh pussy and got excited. She looked over and saw what a minute ago had been four inches of soft penis turn into eight inches of rock-hard dick. She had another orgasm that was so intense, she almost passed out.

When her body stopped trembling, she jumped up and almost fell—her legs were so weak—and ran from the room. She went into the bathroom, cleaned herself up as best she could, and left.

She sat in the car, ashamed at what she had almost done, and said a prayer asking God to forgive her. Finally, she drove home.

A few hours later, Yakki woke up, not even remembering that she had been there. He laid in the bed smiling, trying to remember the dream he was having about Cassie.

"Damn, I miss her ass," he thought. "I can even smell that pussy. I miss her ass so much."

He jumped up, took a quick shower, and got dressed. He locked the house up, got in his car, and drove out to Cedar Creek.

It was after midnight when he made it, and everyone was asleep or inside because the place was quiet. But Em and K-Rock were outside, standing down by the lake when he pulled up. They watched him get out of the car and go inside.

"It was just a matter of time before he brought his ass back," K-Rock said.

"He knew he wasn't going to leave that good-ass Mexi-pussy," Em said, laughing.

"Don't tell me you already hit that?" K-Rock asked.

"Hell no."

"Then how you know it's good?"

"You know how good J-Low's shit is. All Latinos got that good-good."

They heard some giggling, and outta the dark walked J-Low. "Are y'all talking about me?"

"Busted!" K-Rock laughed, pointing at Em.

"Come over here and show me how good my shit is, smart-ass," J-Low told Em.

"You ain't said shit," she said, leading them to a dark spot under some trees.

As soon as Yakki got inside, he could hear the sounds of some serious fucking going on. He followed the sounds to the guest bedroom and eased the door open. Cassie's mom, Marcy, was riding Cassie's dad, reverse cowgirl style. They were fucking so hard, they didn't even notice that he had opened the door. He eased the door back closed and went to the master bedroom.

He opened the door and went in. He could see Cassie lying in bed. When he got closer to the bed, he saw that she wasn't asleep. Her eyes were open, and she was staring at him.

"How you sleeping with all that noise?" he asked.

"I'm not asleep. They've been going at it like that for hours."

"What the hell done got into them?" he asked, laughing.

"Middle age," she said, joining him in laughter.

"I'm sorry, Mami," he said, getting undressed.

"I'm sorry too, Papi. You still gonna marry me? 'Cause I don't want to be a single mother."

"I can't live without you, and you know it. You just make me so fucking mad with that jealous shit."

"I know, Papi, I'm sorry. You took my cherry when I was fourteen. I can't stand to think another woman getting my shit."

"Ain't nobody else getting nothing I got. I don't want nobody but you, Mami," he said, getting in the bed.

"You promise?"

"I promise," he said, hugging her, realizing she was naked. They kissed for a long time.

"You been at your mom's house?"

"Yeah, how you know?"

"You smell like Irish Spring. She's the only one still using that old-ass soap," she said, laughing.

"Don't be making fun of my mama," he said, laughing. "She's just old-school."

"We gonna have a baby."

"You pregnant?"

"Yeah."

He kissed her again while squeezing her ass and pulling her to him.

"I'm naming my son. You not finna name my boy no Hector or Miguel," he said, and they laughed.

"You not finna name my daughter no LaQuita or Shabalika," she said. They laughed harder.

"I love you, Mami."

"I love you too, Papi."

"Can I hit that?" he asked, rubbing her pussy.

"Sí, Papi," she said, climbing on top of him.

Chapter 32

It was over a hundred people gathered in the courtyard at the house in Cedar Creek. Danielle and B-Dub, Cassie and Yakki, Lisa and Brazy, and Glenn and his long-time girlfriend, a Spanish girl named Carmen, were all getting married for the first time.

Omar and Zell, Faye and Pops, George and Kawanna, Smurf and Trina, Cassie's mom and dad, and Chief and Kim were all renewing their vows.

A few weeks earlier, Dub had taken a whole ad out in the paper and asked Danielle, would she marry him. When she saw it, she had tears in her eyes.

Yakki's mom was finally outta rehab and doing good. She had moved in with Yakki and Cassie. She was so happy for her only child, Yakki, that she couldn't stop crying.

They ate fried fish and fries, drank champagne, and smoked weed until the wee hours of the night.

Omar had danced with Danielle most of the night. He was happy for her and Dub. He gave her the keys to the house and told Dub that as soon as he moved out of the other house, to give the keys to Cassie's mom and dad.

Yolonda and Shalika had entertained her sister, Sharonda, and her boyfriend Todd, who Omar knew from back in the day when they were dating Yolonda and Sharonda.

In a few weeks, they were all going to Los Angeles for their wedding. After being high school sweethearts, they were finally getting married.

Todd was also Rudy's best friend. Omar knew that he was going to the wedding for sure in hopes of catching up with Rudy. He wasn't even sure about how he felt about Rudy after the bullshit he pulled. He just really wanted to look him in his eyes and see if Rudy would apologize to him directly, and not over the phone.

The day after everyone left, Omar got up early and went to the home gym to get a workout in. Shalika was already in the gym running on the treadmill.

"Hey," he said, looking at her in her tights. He couldn't help but get excited every time he saw her in something that showed off her figure. She had the most incredible butt he had ever seen.

"Hey, you," she answered, puckering her lips for a kiss. He went over and gave her a quick kiss, but couldn't help but squeeze her ass.

"I knew you were gonna do that," she said matter-of-factly, smiling.

"You reading my mind?"

"Nope, I'm reading him," she said, nodding at his semi-hard-on that was showing in his shorts.

"All these years, and you still do that to me every time I get close to you."

"I hope I never stop doing that to you."

"I hope you don't either."

"I have twenty more minutes. Let me suck that dick?"

"Nope."

"You don't want your dick sucked?"

"Nope, I wanna fuck."

"Oh, okay."

"You have been spending too much time with Yolonda. I've been missing you."

"I can tell," she said, looking down at his shorts where a few minutes ago he had a semi-hard-on that had now turned into a full erection.

"Come on," she said, turning off the treadmill. "He ain't gonna wait."

She took his hand and led him to the shower room in the gym. "Take that off while I rinse this sweat off."

"You better hurry up. I can't wait much longer."

She turned on the water and rinsed off with some coconut-scented body wash. He stood there watching her, mesmerized by how beautiful she was.

When she was finished, she stepped out of the water and asked, "How you want it?" She noticed how he was looking at her and blushed. "What?"

"You are beautiful, thank you," he said, pulling her to him and kissing her deeply.

"Whew, it's been a long time since you've kissed me like that. What are you thanking me for?"

"For being my woman, always holding me down and having my back, and giving me two beautiful kids," he said, kissing her again.

"Three," she said when they finished kissing.

"Three what?" he asked, confused.

"Three beautiful kids."

"You pregnant?"

She nodded, looking at him with a strange look.

"Why you looking like that?" he asked, kissing her again. "You not mad?"

"Hell no. What would I be mad about?"

"I just thought—" He stopped her from talking by kissing her. He sucked on her tongue and nibbled her neck before making his way to her breasts.

"Sit down, I'm finna show you how mad I am. I'm finna suck that pussy."

He not only sucked her pussy, he ate her ass, sucked her toes, and made love to her on the shower floor for over an hour before they exhausted themselves.

Afterwards, they laid there, breathing hard and enjoying the moment.

"I love you, Shalika."

"I love you too."

"This still my pussy?" he asked teasingly.

"Omar, this been your pussy since you signed your name on it January 1st, 2005. I haven't thought about giving this pussy to nobody else. At least not no man. You know I love fucking other women," she said, giggling.

It had been a long time since they had been able to spend some time alone like this, and she was loving it. The last year or so, she had been running back and forth to California with Yolonda, helping her with the music and doing a few commercials, so they never had a chance to spend time alone like this.

"Thank you."

"What are you thanking me for now?" she asked.

"For giving me this good-ass pussy and being the mother of my kids."

"You are welcome, sir," she answered, feeling loved. "But if it's that good, hit it again," she said, rolling on top of him for round two.

Chapter 33

Zell rented a huge RV, and they loaded up on their way to California for the wedding of Todd and Sharonda. They left the kids at home with Danielle, Faye, and Pops.

Zell, Omar, Shalika, Em, K-Rock, J-Low, Chief and Kim, and Pecas and his wife were all in the RV. Yolonda had taken a flight back with Sharonda to help her with the wedding.

They had rented a house on the beach for two weeks. The girls planned on doing some shopping, and they all planned on doing a little sightseeing while they were there. This was the first time Omar had been to the West Coast, so there were a lot of places he wanted to see.

Something had gotten into Omar. He couldn't keep his hands off Shalika. During the ride down, he would stick his tongue out at her when their eyes met, and she would blush, or he would brush up against her on purpose.

Nothing or no one could take the place of Zell or the way he felt about her. She was his soulmate. They thought the same and had a connection that couldn't be matched.

But Shalika had gotten into his blood. Her body and personality had become contagious. He could see it all over her face and in her body language that she was crazy about him. Zell noticed the change in him.

"I thought we were going to lose her."

"Who?"

"Shalika."

"Why you say that?"

"You haven't actually been making her feel wanted. You never spend time with her."

"I live with her."

"You know how we sneak off and make love, or just hang out together? You never do that with her. You only fuck with her when it's all of us together, or her and Yolonda. A woman wants to be with her man alone sometimes."

"You are my wife, and I never want to make you feel uncomfortable."

"You could never do that with her. Trust me, she wouldn't be here if I was uncomfortable. There is no doubt in my mind how you feel about me. I can tell how you make love to me, how you look at me, and how you touch me. You are my man, and I'm your woman. No one can take that place in either of our hearts. I feel you in my soul.

But I saw the way she looked at you when I first met her, and I knew the same way I felt about you, she did too. I also saw that you liked her too, and I felt like if you weren't with me, it would've been her."

"When I went and met her that day, I had no intention of inviting her into our home. But once we started talking, I had such a strong physical attraction to her. I couldn't leave without her coming with me."

"I love her, and I want you to love her just like you love me. Well, not as much as you love me. But, you know what I mean."

"I don't think I could love anyone as much as I love you. You are the only woman I have ever been in love with. I always loved Shalika, but I wasn't in love with her until recently. Something happened. I don't know what it was," he admitted honestly.

"In the gym?" she asked.

"Have y'all been talking about me?" he asked, smiling.

"We don't keep secrets in this house," she said, laughing. "She came to me crying and told me that you made her feel so special. She said that if she would've died that moment, she would have died the happiest woman in the world."

"She said that?"

"Yes, she is crazy about you. She has really had a lonely life, and I want her to have some happiness. You make her happy. We make her happy."

"She's pregnant," he said.

"I know. She wants me to have another baby. I told her, Hell to the NO! Three is enough."

"Look at her," Zell said. "She's beautiful, and that body is amazing. How does her ass just sit up like that? It's like it's just sitting in the air." She shook her head.

"Go fuck her," Zell said.

"Right now?"

"Yes. Take her in the bedroom back there and fuck her. I want to see the look on her face when she comes back out here."

"You don't want to come with us?"

"No, take her back there and fuck the hell out of her."

"You sure?"

"Go," she said, kissing him and going to sit next to J-Low. Omar sat there for a minute until he caught Shalika's eye. He nodded toward the back room and mouthed the words, "I wanna fuck you." She smiled and mouthed back, "Right now?" He nodded and got up, making his way to the bedroom.

When she came in, he was lying on the bed. "Come lay down with me."

"What's wrong?" she asked, laying on the bed with him.

"Nothing is wrong. I just want to hold you for a little while."

"Omar, is everything all right? You're scaring me."

"What you mean?"

"You're loving me so much, you're making my heart feel like it's about to burst."

"I'm sorry I've been neglecting you. But I'm scared too. I'm scared of being hurt and really just being vulnerable or not in control of my feelings. But I'm in love with you."

"Oh my God," she said with tears running down her face.

"Why are you crying?"

"These are happy tears."

"Are you happy?"

"Yes," she whispered.

He wiped her tears away and said, "Give me a kiss then, and I want some sloppy, wet-ass tongue."

She kissed him, and their tongues did a wild dance while they stared into each other's eyes. She was wearing a summer dress, and he pulled it up and slid his hand into her panties, teasing her clit.

"I wanna suck that pussy," he said, licking her juices off his fingers.

"Not this time," she said, helping him lick her juices off his fingers. "I need that dick right now, baby. I can't wait. I need to feel you inside of me. The way you have my heart feeling, I need you inside of me," she added, undressing him and sitting on top of him.

Omar let her set her own rhythm as she rubbed all over his chest, stomach, and face. She leaned forward and planted kisses all over his face, lips, and neck while keeping the same slow rhythm.

After a while, she changed position and turned her back to him, keeping the same slow rhythm. She ground and rolled her hips until she was ready to let go.

"I'm finna cum, baby. Cum with me," she said.

"Let it go, baby," he told her, grabbing her hips and moving in and out of her.

"Oh God, it's coming."

He felt her tighten around him and felt her warm fluids drench his stomach. That pushed him over the edge, and they came together.

After a while, she laid down on the side of him, and they cuddled. She finally got up and went to the bathroom and came back with a warm towel and wiped him clean.

When she was dressed, Omar was sound asleep with a look of complete happiness on his face. She planted a kiss on his lips and quietly left the room, closing the door softly behind her.

Zell winked at her as she came back into the room, and she smiled.

"You look satisfied and happy," Zell told her.

"I am," she said, hugging her.

"Where is he?"

She nodded toward the bedroom. "I put that ass to sleep," she said, and they high-fived.

Chapter 34

Omar and his whole crew were at Todd and Sharonda's house hours before the wedding when Pecas touched him on the shoulder and nodded toward the front door. Rudy had just arrived with a tall black guy.

"There goes Rudy," Em said.

Zell looked up and said, "That's Rudy?"

"Yeah, the Mexican guy," Pecas said.

Zell took off before anyone could stop her. She walked right up to Rudy, hauled off, and slapped the cowboy shit out of him.

"You almost shot me, asshole," she said.

Before anyone could move, Rudy and his friend had five guns pointed at him. Todd, seeing the disturbance, walked over and stepped in front of Rudy.

"Please, Omar, not on my wedding day and in my house in front of my daughter."

"He good. Y'all, put the guns away," Omar said, looking at Rudy with a look that could kill.

"What's going on?" Todd asked.

"Tell him," Omar told Rudy.

"A big misunderstanding," Rudy said, rubbing his face.

"Naw, it wasn't no misunderstanding," Omar said, telling Todd what happened.

"Come on, Rudy, you did that?"

"One of my people did."

"Bro, you owe my wife an apology, right now," Omar told him.

"I sincerely apologize. I hope you can forgive me."

"You need to compensate Sando's family," Zell said.

"I already have."

"For years my husband talked so highly of you. But greed turned you into an animal. Stay away from my family and learn to accept no." She turned and walked away.

"Thank you, Zell," Todd said.

***

Hours later, after the wedding, Omar and Zell sat talking when a beautiful young girl came over and introduced herself.

"Hi, I'm Diamond McGuire. Todd's my father."

"Hi, I'm Zell, and this is my husband Omar." They both shook her hand.

"I know who you are. Aunt Shalika talks so much about you guys, I feel like I already know you. Did you enjoy the wedding?"

"Yes, it was beautiful," Zell said.

"I'm so happy for my dad. He finally married his childhood sweetheart. Thanks for coming, Aunt Zell and Uncle Omar," she said before leaving to go talk to other guests.

"That's a pretty little girl," Omar said.

"She is, and smart too. She adores her dad."

Omar watched as Rudy hugged Sharonda and Todd and left out the front door with his friend.

"I can't believe he did that," Omar said, shaking his head.

"I can't either. But that's what money and greed will do to some people. He seemed sincere in his apology."

"Oh, I think he was. That was like one of my best friends."

"It's over now. Don't even think about him. Let's have another drink and dance," she said.

"Come on, I wanna feel on that booty anyway," he said as an R. Kelly song came over the speakers.

"I hope that's not all you want to do to this booty," she said.

"I'ma hurt that when we get back to the crib."

"I want you to," she said, putting her arms around his neck and moving her body against his to the music.

Omar felt someone behind him and looked back. Shalika was behind him. They both started grinding against him.

"I wanna get mine hurt too," she said, laughing.

"I'ma fuck the shit outta both of y'all."

"Yeah, yeah, yeah, talk is cheap," Zell said, and they high-fived.

Epilogue

Rudy and Kenyatta walked out the house and headed to the car.

"Bro, what the fuck was you thinkin', havin' them niggas take a shot at the nigga wife?" Kenyatta asked.

"It was an accident. Freddy did that shit," Rudy said as they got in the car and closed the doors.

They both heard the familiar sound of a gun cocking behind them and looked back.

They saw George sitting in the back seat, holding a pistol with an extended clip.

"Sup, Blood," George said.

To be continued…

The Lane 4
Coming Soon!

Lock Down Publications and Ca$h Presents
Assisted Publishing Packages

Due to an increase in the price of services we have increased our prices. The prices below reflect the price increase as of 11/1/24.

BASIC PACKAGE $699 Editing Cover Design Formatting	UPGRADED PACKAGE $1000 Typing Editing Cover Design Formatting Upload eBooks to Amazon Upload Paperback to Amazon
ADVANCE PACKAGE $1,400 Typing Editing (line editing/content) Cover Design Formatting Copyright Registration Proofreading Upload eBooks to Amazon Upload Paperback to Amazon	LDP SUPREME PACKAGE $1,700 Typing Editing (line editing/content) Cover Design Formatting Copyright Registration Proofreading Set up Amazon Account Upload eBooks to Amazon Upload Paperback to Amazon Advertise on LDP's Amazon and Facebook Page

***

Other services available upon request.
Additional charges may apply

Lock Down Publications
P.O. Box 944
Stockbridge, GA 30281-9998
Phone: 470 303-9761
Email: lockdownpublications@gmail.com

153

Submission Guideline

Submit the first three chapters of your completed manuscript to ldpsubmissions@gmail.com. In the subject line add **Your Book's Title**. The manuscript must be in a Word Doc file and sent as an attachment. Document should be in Times New Roman, double spaced, and in size 12 font. Also, provide your synopsis and full contact information. If sending multiple submissions, they must each be in a separate email.

Have a story but no way to send it electronically? You can still submit to LDP/Ca$h Presents. Send in the first three chapters, written or typed, of your completed manuscript to:

LDP: Submissions Dept
P.O. Box 944
Stockbridge, GA 30281-9998

DO NOT send original manuscript. Must be a duplicate. Provide your synopsis and a cover letter containing your full contact information.

Thanks for considering LDP and Ca$h Presents.

NEW RELEASES

BLOODLINE OF A SAVAGE 1-3
THESE VICIOUS STREETS 1-3
RELENTLESS GOON 1-3
BY PRINCE A. TAUHID

THE BUTTERFLY MAFIA 1-3
BY FUMIYA PAYNE

A THUG'S STREET PRINCESS 1&2
BY MEESHA

CITY OF SMOKE 3
BY MOLOTTI

GET IT IN SLUGS 1 &2
BY B. STALL

STANDING ON HER BUSINESS 1&2
BY DG SANTANA

STEPPERS 1,2&3
THE REAL BADDIES OF CHI-RAQ
BY KING RIO

THE LANE 1&2
BY KEN-KEN SPENCE

THUG OF SPADES 1&2
LOVE IN THE TRENCHES 2
CORNER BOYS
BY COREY ROBINSON

TIL DEATH 3
BY ARYANNA

THE LANE 3 | KEN-KEN SPENCE

THE BIRTH OF A GANGSTER 4
BY DELMONT PLAYER

PRODUCT OF THE STREETS 1-3
BY DEMOND "MONEY" ANDERSON

NO TIME FOR ERROR
BY KEESE

MONEY HUNGRY DEMONS 1-2
BY TRANAY ADAMS

HUB CITY MENACE 1-3
BY J. WHITE

A THUGGISH PASSION 1&2
LAND OF DA HOOLIGANZ 1-4
KILLAZ ON STANDBY 1&2
BY IRA B.

FO'EVA ROLLIN 1&2
BY ASSA RAYMOND BAKER

THE LEVEL UP 1&3
BY LUXURY KING

Coming Soon from Lock Down Publications/Ca$h Presents

IF YOU CROSS ME ONCE 6
ANGEL V
By Anthony Fields

A THUGS STREET PRINCESS 3
By Meesha

CORNER BOYS 2
By Corey Robinson

THA TAKEOVER
By Keith Chandler

BETRAYAL OF A G 2
By Ray Vinci

SAVAGE FAMILY EMPIRE 1&2
SOULLESS GOON 1,2&3
THE DIRTY SIDE OF MONEY 1,2&3
By Prince

FOR MY ENEMY'S SAKE
AMBITIONS OF A SLIDER
FRESH OFF DA PORCH
By IRA B.

BY THE TRUCKLOAD 1-4
TIPPIN' THE SCALES 1-3
BAD BITCHES WIT GUNZ 3
PROBLEM SOLVED 2
By Christopher "Diesel" Hornezes

Available Now

RESTRAINING ORDER 1 & 2
By **CA$H & Coffee**

LOVE KNOWS NO BOUNDARIES 1-3
By **Coffee**

RAISED AS A GOON I, II, III & IV
BRED BY THE SLUMS I, II, III
BLAST FOR ME I & II
ROTTEN TO THE CORE I II III
A BRONX TALE I, II, III
DUFFLE BAG CARTEL I II III IV V VI
HEARTLESS GOON I II III IV V
A SAVAGE DOPEBOY I II
DRUG LORDS I II III
CUTTHROAT MAFIA I II
KING OF THE TRENCHES
By **Ghost**

LAY IT DOWN I & II
LAST OF A DYING BREED I II
BLOOD STAINS OF A SHOTTA I & II III
By **Jamaica**

LOYAL TO THE GAME I II III
LIFE OF SIN I, II III
By **TJ & Jelissa**

IF LOVING HIM IS WRONG…I & II
LOVE ME EVEN WHEN IT HURTS I II III
By **Jelissa**

PUSH IT TO THE LIMIT
By **Bre' Hayes**

THE LANE 3 | KEN-KEN SPENCE

BLOODY COMMAS I & II
SKI MASK CARTEL I, II & III
KING OF NEW YORK I II, III IV V
RISE TO POWER I II III
COKE KINGS I II III IV V
BORN HEARTLESS I II III IV
KING OF THE TRAP I II
By **T.J. Edwards**

WHEN THE STREETS CLAP BACK I & II III
THE HEART OF A SAVAGE I II III IV
MONEY MAFIA I II
LOYAL TO THE SOIL I II III
By **Jibril Williams**

A DISTINGUISHED THUG STOLE MY HEART I II & III
LOVE SHOULDN'T HURT I II III IV
RENEGADE BOYS 1-4
PAID IN KARMA 1-3
SAVAGE STORMS 1-3
AN UNFORESEEN LOVE 1-3
BABY, I'M WINTERTIME COLD 1-3
A THUG'S STREET PRINCESS 1&2
By **Meesha**

A GANGSTER'S CODE 1-3
A GANGSTER'S SYN 1-3
THE SAVAGE LIFE 1-3
CHAINED TO THE STREETS 1-3
BLOOD ON THE MONEY 1-3
A GANGSTA'S PAIN 1-3
BEAUTIFUL LIES AND UGLY TRUTHS
CHURCH IN THESE STREETS
By **J-Blunt**

CUM FOR ME 1-8
An LDP Erotica Collaboration

THE LANE 3 | KEN-KEN SPENCE

BLOOD OF A BOSS 1-5
SHADOWS OF THE GAME
TRAP BASTARD
By **Askari**

THE STREETS BLEED MURDER 1-3
THE HEART OF A GANGSTA 1-3
By **Jerry Jackson**

WHEN A GOOD GIRL GOES BAD
By **Adrienne**

THE COST OF LOYALTY 1-3
By **Kweli**

BRIDE OF A HUSTLA 1-3
THE FETTI GIRLS 1-3
CORRUPTED BY A GANGSTA 1-4
BLINDED BY HIS LOVE
THE PRICE YOU PAY FOR LOVE 1-3
DOPE GIRL MAGIC 1-3
By **Destiny Skai**

A KINGPIN'S AMBITION
A KINGPIN'S AMBITION II
I MURDER FOR THE DOUGH
By **Ambitious**

TRUE SAVAGE 1-7
DOPE BOY MAGIC 1-3
MIDNIGHT CARTEL 1-3
CITY OF KINGZ 1&2
NIGHTMARE ON SILENT AVE
THE PLUG OF LIL MEXICO 1&2
CLASSIC CITY
By **Chris Green**

THE LANE 3 | KEN-KEN SPENCE

A GANGSTER'S REVENGE 1-4
THE BOSS MAN'S DAUGHTERS 1-5
A SAVAGE LOVE 1&2
BAE BELONGS TO ME 1&2
A HUSTLER'S DECEIT 1-3
WHAT BAD BITCHES DO 1-3
SOUL OF A MONSTER 1-3
KILL ZONE
A DOPE BOY'S QUEEN 1-3
TIL DEATH 1-3
IMMA DIE BOUT MINE 1-6
DYING FOR LIKES
By **Aryanna**

A DOPEBOY'S PRAYER
By **Eddie "Wolf" Lee**

THE KING CARTEL 1-3
By **Frank Gresham**

THESE NIGGAS AIN'T LOYAL 1-3
By **Nikki Tee**

GANGSTA SHYT 1-3
By **CATO**

THE ULTIMATE BETRAYAL
By **Phoenix**

BOSS'N UP 1-3
By **Royal Nicole**

I LOVE YOU TO DEATH
By **Destiny J**

I RIDE FOR MY HITTA
I STILL RIDE FOR MY HITTA
By **Misty Holt**

THE LANE 3 | KEN-KEN SPENCE

LOVE & CHASIN' PAPER
By **Qay Crockett**

TO DIE IN VAIN
SINS OF A HUSTLA
By **ASAD**

BROOKLYN HUSTLAZ
By **Boogsy Morina**

BROOKLYN ON LOCK 1 & 2
By **Sonovia**

GANGSTA CITY
By **Teddy Duke**

A DRUG KING AND HIS DIAMOND 1-3
A DOPEMAN'S RICHES
HER MAN, MINE'S TOO 1&2
CASH MONEY HO'S
THE WIFEY I USED TO BE 1&2
PRETTY GIRLS DO NASTY THINGS
By **Nicole Goosby**

LIPSTICK KILLAH 1-3
CRIME OF PASSION 1-3
FRIEND OR FOE 1-3
By **Mimi**

TRAPHOUSE KING 1-3
KINGPIN KILLAZ 1-3
STREET KINGS 1&2
PAID IN BLOOD 1&2
CARTEL KILLAZ 1-3
DOPE GODS 1&2
By **Hood Rich**

THE STREETS ARE CALLING
By **Duquie Wilson**

STEADY MOBBN' 1-3
THE STREETS STAINED MY SOUL 1-3
By **Marcellus Allen**

WHO SHOT YA 1-3
SON OF A DOPE FIEND 1-4
HEAVEN GOT A GHETTO 1&2
SKI MASK MONEY 1&2
By **Renta**

GORILLAZ IN THE BAY 1-4
TEARS OF A GANGSTA 1/&2
3X KRAZY 1&2
STRAIGHT BEAST MODE 1&2
By **DE'KARI**

TRIGGADALE 1-3
MURDA WAS THE CASE 1-3
By **Elijah R. Freeman**

SLAUGHTER GANG 1-3
RUTHLESS HEART 1-3
By **Willie Slaughter**

GOD BLESS THE TRAPPERS 1-3
THESE SCANDALOUS STREETS 1-3
FEAR MY GANGSTA 1-5
THESE STREETS DON'T LOVE NOBODY 1-2
BURY ME A G 1-5
A GANGSTA'S EMPIRE 1-4
THE DOPEMAN'S BODYGAURD 1&2
THE REALEST KILLAZ 1-3
THE LAST OF THE OGS 1-3
By **Tranay Adams**

MARRIED TO A BOSS 1-3
By **Destiny Skai & Chris Green**

KINGZ OF THE GAME 1-7
CRIME BOSS 1-4
By **Playa Ray**

FUK SHYT
By **Blakk Diamond**

DON'T F#CK WITH MY HEART 1&2
By **Linnea**

ADDICTED TO THE DRAMA 1-3
IN THE ARM OF HIS BOSS
By **Jamila**

LOYALTY AIN'T PROMISED 1&2
By **Keith Williams**

YAYO 1-4
A SHOOTER'S AMBITION 1&2
BRED IN THE GAME
By **S. Allen**

TRAP GOD 1-3
RICH $AVAGE 1-3
MONEY IN THE GRAVE 1-3
CARTEL MONEY 1&2
By **Martell Troublesome Bolden**

FOREVER GANGSTA 1&2
GLOCKS ON SATIN SHEETS 1&2
By **Adrian Dulan**

TOE TAGZ 1-4
LEVELS TO THIS SHYT 1&2
IT'S JUST ME AND YOU
By **Ah'Million**

THE LANE 3 | KEN-KEN SPENCE

KINGPIN DREAMS 1-3
RAN OFF ON DA PLUG
By **Paper Boi Rari**

THE STREETS MADE ME 1-3
By **Larry D. Wright**

CONFESSIONS OF A GANGSTA 1-4
CONFESSIONS OF A JACKBOY 1-3
CONFESSIONS OF A HITMAN
CONFESSIONS OF A DOPE BOY
By **Nicholas Lock**

I'M NOTHING WITHOUT HIS LOVE
SINS OF A THUG
TO THE THUG I LOVED BEFORE
A GANGSTA SAVED XMAS
IN A HUSTLER I TRUST
By **Monet Dragun**

QUIET MONEY 1-3
THUG LIFE 1-3
EXTENDED CLIP 1&2
A GANGSTA'S PARADISE
By **Trai'Quan**

CAUGHT UP IN THE LIFE 1-3
THE STREETS NEVER LET GO 1-3
By **Robert Baptiste**

NEW TO THE GAME 1-3
MONEY, MURDER & MEMORIES 1-3
By **Malik D. Rice**

CREAM 2-3
THE STREETS WILL TALK
By **Yolanda Moore**

THE LANE 3 | KEN-KEN SPENCE

THE STREETS WILL NEVER CLOSE 1-3
By **K'ajji**

LIFE OF A SAVAGE 1-4
A GANGSTA'S QUR'AN 1-4
MURDA SEASON 1-3
GANGLAND CARTEL 1-3
CHI'RAQ GANGSTAS 1-4
KILLERS ON ELM STREET 1-3
JACK BOYZ N DA BRONX 1-3
A DOPEBOY'S DREAM 1-3
JACK BOYS VS DOPE BOYS 1-3
COKE GIRLZ
COKE BOYS
SOSA GANG 1&2
BRONX SAVAGES
BODYMORE KINGPINS
BLOOD OF A GOON
By **Romell Tukes**

CONCRETE KILLA 1-3
VICIOUS LOYALTY 1-3
BLOODY MONEY BAGS
By **Kingpen**

THE ULTIMATE SACRIFICE 1-6
KHADIFI
IF YOU CROSS ME ONCE 1-3
ANGEL 1-4
IN THE BLINK OF AN EYE
By **Anthony Fields**

THE LIFE OF A HOOD STAR
By **Ca$h & Rashia Wilson**

NIGHTMARES OF A HUSTLA 1-3
BLOOD AND GAMES 1&2
By **King Dream**

166

THE LANE 3 | KEN-KEN SPENCE

GHOST MOB
By **Stilloan Robinson**

HARD AND RUTHLESS 1&2
MOB TOWN 251
THE BILLIONAIRE BENTLEYS 1-3
REAL G'S MOVE IN SILENCE
By **Von Diesel**

MOB TIES 1-7
SOUL OF A HUSTLER, HEART OF A KILLER 1-3
GORILLAZ IN THE TRENCHES
OOPS CRY TOO 1&2
THE DAUGHTER OF A CARTEL BOSS
By **SayNoMore**

BODYMORE MURDERLAND 1-3
THE BIRTH OF A GANGSTER 1-4
By **Delmont Player**

FOR THE LOVE OF A BOSS 1&2
By **C. D. Blue**

KILLA KOUNTY 1-5
TENDER
By **Khufu**

MOBBED UP 1-4
THE BRICK MAN 1-5
THE COCAINE PRINCESS 1-10
STEPPERS 1-3
SUPER GREMLIN 1-4
A GANGSTA'S SON
By **King Rio**

MONEY GAME 1&2
By **Smoove Dolla**

THE LANE 3 | KEN-KEN SPENCE

A GANGSTA'S KARMA 1-5
By **FLAME**

KING OF THE TRENCHES 1-3
By **GHOST & TRANAY ADAMS**

BAD BITCHES WIT GUNZ 1&2
PROBLEM SOLVED
By "Christopher Diesel" Hornezes

QUEEN OF THE ZOO 1&2
By **Black Migo**

GRIMEY WAYS 1-3
BETRAYAL OF A G
By **Ray Vinci**

XMAS WITH AN ATL SHOOTER
By **Ca$h & Destiny Skai**

KING KILLA 1&2
By **Vincent "Vitto" Holloway**

BETRAYAL OF A THUG 1&2
By **Fre$h**

COUNTDOWN OF A KILLA 1&2
SEX, MURDER AND GOD 1&2
GUNS DOWN, BOTTOMS UP 1&2
By Lo-Life

THE MURDER QUEENS 1-7
By **Michael Gallon**

FOR THE LOVE OF BLOOD 1-4
By **Jamel Mitchell**

THE LANE 3 | KEN-KEN SPENCE

HOOD CONSIGLIERE 1&2
NO TIME FOR ERROR
By **Keese**

PROTÉGÉ OF A LEGEND 1,2&3
LOVE IN THE TRENCHES 1&2
By **Corey Robinson**

THE PLUG'S RUTHLESS DAUGHTER 1&2
By **Tony Daniels**

BORN IN THE GRAVE 1-3
CRIME PAYS
By **Self Made Tay**

MOAN IN MY MOUTH
By **XTASY**

TORN BETWEEN A GANGSTER AND A GENTLEMAN
By **J-BLUNT & Miss Kim**

LOYALTY IS EVERYTHING 1-3
CITY OF SMOKE 1-3
By **Molotti**

HERE TODAY GONE TOMORROW 1&2
By **Fly Rock**

WOMEN LIE MEN LIE 1-4
FIFTY SHADES OF SNOW 1-3
STACK BEFORE YOU SPLURGE
GIRLS FALL LIKE DOMINOES
NAÏVE TO THE STREETS
By **ROY MILLIGAN**

PILLOW PRINCESS
By **S. Hawkins**

THE LANE 3 | KEN-KEN SPENCE

THE BUTTERFLY MAFIA 1-3
SALUTE MY SAVAGERY 1&2
By **Fumiya Payne**

THE LANE 1&2
By Ken-Ken Spence

THE PUSSY TRAP 1-5
By **Nene Capri**

DIRTY DNA
By **Blaque**

SANCTIFIED AND HORNY
by **XTASY**

BOOKS BY LDP'S CEO, CA$H

TRUST IN NO MAN
TRUST IN NO MAN 2
TRUST IN NO MAN 3
BONDED BY BLOOD
SHORTY GOT A THUG
THUGS CRY
THUGS CRY 2
THUGS CRY 3
TRUST NO BITCH
TRUST NO BITCH 2
TRUST NO BITCH 3
TIL MY CASKET DROPS
RESTRAINING ORDER
RESTRAINING ORDER 2
IN LOVE WITH A CONVICT
LIFE OF A HOOD STAR
XMAS WITH AN ATL SHOOTER